For Christopher

ALSO IN THIS SERIES:

Death Master

You Will Die

Total Wipeout

Deep Cut

Coming Soon:

Vanished Children

ACKNOWLEDGMENTS

Edited: David Burton

Cover image: SelfPubBookCovers .com/ Visions

CCBC
AMAZON
10/2019

A WATERY GRAVE

Sweat-soaked hair clung like fingers to his head. Pounding pressure threatened to burst his skull into a million tiny shards. Raging thirst razored his throat, leaving him dizzy and groggy, as he melted in and out of consciousness. Images and moments swirled, merging into a timeless, mashed-up surreality. His body spasmed from the pain of being in one position for far too long.

Each time his consciousness returned, it would stay a little longer. Things were becoming more clear. He tried to hold onto the clarity, to remember how he had ended up here. The last thing he could recall was stumbling his way home after a night out with his friends. He'd had a bust-up with his girlfriend, Wendy. Smiling, cursing, maddening Wendy. He would give anything to see her again. Hold her in his arms. Tell her he was sorry. Kiss her wild, mousy hair and stare into her fiery amber eyes. But, he was inside a bag. A cloth sack. Upside down.

Two tiny holes allowed a fuzzy image of foliage, a river

bank and water. He was close to the water. Too close. The earthy, dead-fish stench filled his prison.

His breathing hot and heavy in his ears, he shook his head in an attempt to clear it and called out.

"Hello? Is anybody there?"

The only answer was the whisper of water over stone. His friends would be back any moment. He was sure of that. They had obviously thought this funny. It wasn't funny anymore.

Then came the gut-clenching realisation he was sinking. Coming ever closer to the water. The smell and the coldness overwhelming, he drew in a sharp, rasping breath.

"No! No! Please... Lads, I give in. You got me. Boys..."

The water continued rising up his head, until he assumed a foetal position within the bag. Any respite was short-lived. It hit his neck and shoulders, just before his next words became a warbled noise. It carried on up, relentless.

The bag threshed about for several minutes, before finally falling still. The observer waited another few minutes, before pulling the bag back up a little to cut the rope which had tied his victim in. The lifeless form plunged back into the water, slowly sinking, head first.

When he was sure his victim had disappeared, he rolled up the cloth sack and left the scene.

2

CURIOSITY KILLED THE CAT

Yvonne watched the rubber-suited divers reel the body in, painstakingly loading it onto the berry-red rescue dinghy. Their gentle reverence impressed her. Checked shirt and jeans became a dark-haired, young, adult male.

She rubbed her chin, staring hard. If they'd been on land, he'd be photographed *in situ,* the area cordoned off while SOCO worked it. Water had no respect for forensic process. Rope and rubber dinghies were your lot, until hauled in to dry land. They had a good idea who it was. Lloyd Jones had gone missing some days before. They wouldn't be sure, however, until formal identification had taken place.

Pathologist Roger Hanson barked instruction to his assistants, as he made his way to where the body lay stretchered. She held her breath. This wasn't her case. At least, not yet. Curiosity had brought her down here. This was the second body to be found on this stretch of the river in as many months. Not unheard of, but definitely not the usual.

"I knew I'd find you here." Dewi grinned, teasing accusation narrowing his eyes as he made his way along the bank.

"Are you calling me nosey?" Yvonne pulled a face.

"Er...Yeah." Dewi laughed then grunted, as he remembered the sober occasion. "Drunk, I'd imagine." He pressed his lips into a thin line. "Young."

"Yes." Yvonne headed in the direction of Hanson and his team. Dewi followed.

A gloved and plastic-suited Hanson waited patiently for the dinghy to moor. "Probably fell in after a few," he said, by way of greeting. "Can't see any obvious trauma on the body."

"We had another body a few weeks back." The DI's hands were on her hips as she gazed down. "Hadn't expected one again, so soon."

"It's the heat. Town centre's been a bit busier than usual," he answered, referring to the summer revellers.

"How soon will you know cause of death?"

Hanson looked down at the water, then back at Yvonne. "Should be able to say for sure within about forty-eight hours or so, provided toxicology pull their finger out."

Yvonne knelt next to the dead man. He lay, a pale ghost on the stretcher, river detritus in his matted hair. The skin on his hands was severely wrinkled. His stomach had begun to swell.

Yvonne's thoughts turned to his friends and family. The news would hit them like a punch to the chest. No. A baseball bat to the head. The raining of blows from some dark power, unseen. The removal from beneath of everything solid. Having personally felt that mind-numbing, knee-buckling sense of loss, more than once, she didn't envy the officers who'd be knocking on their door.

"Ay-up, here comes Carwyn." Dewi nodded in the direction of one of the divers, who was headed their way. "Carwyn Davies. It's been a while."

The diver freed his head from his rubber suit and wiped his brow. "Dewi." He nodded back. Then, looking from Dewi to Yvonne and back, said, "It's probably not a murder, you know."

Dewi grinned, "It's okay, we're just taking a look."

Yvonne pulled at her bottom lip. "What makes you so sure it's not murder? There's been no autopsy yet."

Carwyn shrugged. "He'd been drinking. We found his mobile phone upstream and marks where he'd most probably slipped down the bank. His family said he'd phoned them, telling them he was lost. Most likely disorientated. His phone went dead during the call. Looks like he was concentrating on talking to them, when he fell into the water. If he was drunk, it would've made it hard to get out. The river's very swollen and fast-flowing."

"The place where you found the phone, is it marked out?" Yvonne put her hands in her pockets, frown lines creasing her forehead.

"Er, yeah. We've got it cordoned off. Forensics took a look where he fell. It's been photographed already."

"Great."

Carwyn grimaced. "Look, I'd better be going. Nice to see you, Dewi. And good to meet you...er..."

"Yvonne."

"Yvonne," he nodded.

"She's my DI." Dewi grinned.

"Ma'am." Carwyn coloured.

"It's okay. Thanks for the info, Carwyn."

"Better get back to the station, then?" Dewi eyed the lines on Yvonne's forehead. "Still thinking?"

She shrugged."No. No, let's go." She took her hands out

of her jacket pockets and headed back with him the way they had come. They had more than enough to be getting on with.

LATER THAT EVENING, she was back, standing at the blue-and-white, police cordon by the river. It was hard to associate the peace of this place with death, filled as it was with the sounds of lapping water and summer birdsong. After he had fallen in, the air would have been full of desperation, as he clawed around for anything to hold on to. Except, nothing would prevent the inevitable. She closed her eyes, and it was several seconds before she opened them again.

She could see the flattened trails where the young man's feet had supposedly lost their grip. The place he had dropped his phone. Had his parents heard a splash before the phone went dead? She would check when she got back to the station.

Peering down, large boulders peppered the shoreline, where the river abutted the bank. He would have had to have hit those on the way down. She took a couple of pictures with her mobile. She expected his body would be bruised, perhaps with a broken bone or two from the fall onto those rocks. She could look out for that when the autopsy results came through.

Glancing around, she wondered how he got here. If this really was where he went in, he was half a mile away from the town centre. She had read the 'missing' articles in the County Times, which described how he had left the Elephant and Castle public house on Broad Street, near the main bridge, and had told friends he was headed to his parents home on Canal Road, barely a thousand metres away. He would have accessed the riverside path via some steep steps down and then headed right, along the river path, in the direction of Canal Road. So why, then, was his body found upstream, as though he had reached the path and turned left, heading in the direction alongside and behind the town car park? It didn't make sense unless he was so inebriated that he had lost all sense of direction. Had he been distracted by something, or someone, and headed that way to investigate?

She thought about picking her way further down the bank, but decided against it. Instead, she headed back up, still deep in thought.

Something caught her eye. To her left, the thick trunk of an ash tree had been chalked with two vertical lines, equal in length. She cast her eyes around but could see no markings on any other tree in the area. She took a couple more pictures with her mobile.

ANATOMY OF A DROWNING

Yvonne paused to listen outside LLewellyn's office door before giving it a couple of clipped raps. She could barely hear his answer. He must have his head buried in something.

He looked up from his papers as she entered, his head cocking to one side. "Yvonne? Everything okay?"

The DI cleared her throat. "Sir, I wanted to speak to you about the drowning in the river. The body was pulled out yesterday."

"Yes. Sad business."

"I'd like to look into it a little."

"Oh? I thought it was an accidental death?"

"Well, there's a possibility it was a suicide and there's some confusion around where, exactly, the victim went in. It's almost certain he didn't go in where his phone was found, though there were imprints indicting he had slipped, there."

"Okay-"

The DI tapped her pen several times on her chin. "He

was in conversation with his family. For the sake of completion, I'd like to talk to them and find out what was said."

The DCI grunted. "Sounds perfectly sensible. Don't spend too much time on it, though, Yvonne, you have to prioritise the hit-and-run."

Yvonne's stomach turned over. For just a little while today, she had allowed the hit-and-run to hide on the backburner of her mind. It returned with full force, full clarity and gut-wrenching sadness. A twelve-year-old boy was mown down outside his school on Plantation Lane. The driver had carried on going. The two children who had witnessed the incident had described a white or silver car, possibly an urban four-by-four, but knew neither the model nor the registration. All they could say was the car had taken a right turn at the bottom of the lane and was being driven at speed. The DI had eaten, drunk and slept the case for two weeks but was really no further forward.

"It's okay, I know the case isn't easy." Llewellyn sensed her sadness and frustration. "Everyone wants closure and the press won't leave us alone until we have it. Keep digging."

AUTOPSY

~

Hanson's autopsy of Lloyd Jones was underway as Yvonne suited up and entered the brightly lit mortuary.

He gave her a brief glance, as she finished putting on her over-shoes. "Eyes were wide and glistening, when he came out of the river."

"Fear?"

"Confirms he died in the water. He wasn't killed beforehand."

"I see." Yvonne rubbed her chin. "How drunk was he?"

"Well, that's where I am somewhat perplexed."

"Go on."

"Aside from minor bruising, and very minor abrasions, there's no injury."

"So, very drunk?"

"No. He was two and half times the legal limit for driving. Drunk, but not so drunk he couldn't put up a fight to survive. I'd have expected maybe a few torn muscles from the struggle to stay afloat and, given where he was found, a fistful of debris."

"Grabbed whilst he was trying to stay afloat."

Hanson nodded. "A drowning man really does clutch at straws."

"Did he commit suicide?"

"That's very possible. Everything else we see would fit that hypothesis. He was found in a semi-foetal position. Head-down and still submerged. It's possible he was beginning to rise but decomposition was only just getting started. His blood had settled where we would expect and there was nothing at all to suggest foul play."

"Did you see where he was supposed to have gone in?" Yvonne folded her arms, leaning back against an empty trolley.

"No, not yet."

"It's full of rocks. Boulders, actually. If he'd slipped down that bank, I'd have expected him to be severely bruised. May I?" The DI took her mobile phone to the pathologist, to show him her photographs of the slip marks on the bank and the rocks below.

Hanson pursed his lips. "He didn't fall in there. Definitely not. There's nothing I see that would support it."

"It's where his phone was found. He'd been in conversation with his parents."

Hanson shook his head. "Strange."

Yvonne nodded. "Something's off."

"Unless he fell there, picked himself up, but couldn't find his phone. Then, maybe he wandered about and fell in somewhere else?"

"Hmm." The DI pocketed her mobile phone. "There was drowning a few weeks ago, wasn't there?"

"Now, that one I believe was accidental. The guy was

four or five times over the limit and a disaster waiting to happen. He was using the river walk as a shortcut but was the wrong side of it. Looked like he tried to swim across and was overcome before he made it. The river's running so fast, right now."

"Would you mind if I came back to you for more details on that drowning, if I need to?"

"Be my guest."

"Did you run a full toxicology for this victim?" Yvonne gestured towards the dead man.

"We did. Nothing detected aside from the alcohol."

"Poor bugger.' Yvonne sighed, her glistening eyes lingering on the young man's lifeless face.

"Indeed."

"Well, I'll leave you to it." She gave the pathologist a weak smile, before turning for the door. "Let me know if you find anything else unusual."

THE YOUNG MAN *fitted the bill: lean, athletic, bright. He was animatedly relating a story to his two friends, all of them laughing. His beer spilled a little in the telling. The room, in the Lion public house, was filling up, but not so full that he didn't have a clear view of his would-be-prey. Not yet, anyway.*

He placed a trembling hand into his jacket pocket to feel the tiny, glass vial, taking a deep breath and letting it out slowly, as he confirmed it was still there. He moved forward to stand next to the laughing group, right in front of the bar.

"Get you anything?" The teenage barman enquired, finishing drying off a glass, before putting it on a shelf below the bar.

"Just a swift half. I'm only passing through." He managed a half smile, though his mental focus was taken up by the young

man in the white cotton shirt, whose muscular frame stretched the material, but not too much.

"There you go, sir. That'll be one pound and forty."

He felt in his pocket for the change, handing over one-pound-fifty, holding his hand up when the barman tried to hand him the ten pence change.

He glanced around the room, near the ceiling. One CCTV camera, probably with a fish-eye lens, taking in the whole room at once. Perhaps it wasn't going to be possible tonight. He couldn't afford to be caught on camera.

"Be right back." His quarry ran a hand through his dark hair, before heading to the gents. He'd left the last third of his drink on a ledge, against the wall. Next to it were a bunch of stacked stools. The young man's friends availed themselves of three of them and moved away from the bar area.

"Could I have a whisky?"

The barman nodded and muttered, "Sure. Coming right up," before turning his back.

The hunter walked over to the stack of stools and, with his back to the room, whipped out the vial, emptying its contents into the young man's drink. He then grabbed a stool and headed to a free space, near the door. As far as the camera could see, he was merely getting a stool. Not that they would detect any spiking. The GHB would be out of his quarry's system well before he was found.

The young man was back, taking his beer from the ledge, quickly sighting his friends and grabbing the waiting seat.

He wanted to watch but couldn't risk it.

"Come on, drink up," the larger of the two friends instructed. One more and we'll move on. I fancy another at The Castle."

"All right, keep your hair on." The quarry downed the rest of his drink and grabbed his jacket. As they left the Lion, the young man stumbled on the step.

Not yet, it was too soon. *The hunter gritted his teeth then relaxed, as he realised the boy was walking fine, now. Just a little tipsy.*

I*T WAS HALF-AN-HOUR LATER, the young man stumbled down the Castle Vaults steps, into the alleyway. The nearest bouncer was in the middle of dealing with a fight that had just kicked off and didn't see him go.*

The hunter stayed back, knowing by now his quarry would be feeling worse for wear and wanting to get home. He followed at a distance, avoiding, where he could, the CCTV cameras. The young man's home was a few streets away. He overtook him and headed in that direction, resisting the urge to make contact or say something. He had to trust that home was where the guy was headed. There was no CCTV where the van was parked. The boy would be coming that way and would offer little resistance. Not now the drug would be in full swing. A swift u-turn and they'd be heading up the Milford Road and out of town. He'd gotten false plates on the van, just in case.

5

YOUNG LIVES LOST

"Finish up that coffee and come with me."

"Ma'am?" Dewi gulped down the dregs and grabbed his jacket, barely having time to get it on before they were heading out of the station. "Where are we going?"

"We have two families to visit."

Dewi shrugged and got into the passenger seat. "Right," was all he said, though he raised an eyebrow at his DI driving faster than usual. Especially given she was saying so little.

A PALE, young woman, of around seventeen, opened the door to the tiny cottage on Canal Road. Yvonne introduced herself and Dewi, and the young woman confirmed she was Hannah Jones, sister of Lloyd Jones, the victim they had observed being pulled from the river.

"My dad's out," she added, "but my mum, Margaret, is inside."

The DI took in the tousled hair and red eyes, eyelashes still glistening with wiped-away tears. "Hannah, I'm so sorry for your loss. May we come in?"

Hannah nodded and stepped back. "Mum," she called, as she moved through the hall. "We've got some police officers here to see us about Lloyd."

"Oh." Margaret Jones was wide-eyed, as she came to the hall. "You'd better come in." She led the way through to a living room, so small that four seemed almost too many people for the room.

Mrs Jones held her hand towards the sofa, for them to sit down. She perched on the arm of the sofa, seemingly lost and unsure what to do. Hannah stood beside the tiny, empty fireplace, hands on hips.

The DI took out her pocketbook. "Is it alright if we ask you a few questions?"

Mrs Jones nodded. "Was it an accident? They're saying he fell in." She put her hand over her mouth in a futile attempt to hold back a sob.

"We could find no signs of foul-play. We've come to ask you how your son had been feeling in himself...prior to his night out?"

"You don't think he did this on purpose, do you?" Hannah interjected, her body stiff. Mrs Jones stifled another sob.

"We don't know. It's one possibility we're considering."

"He wouldn't." Hannah was emphatic. "Someone pushed him in."

"He was nineteen, wasn't he?"

Margaret Jones nodded.

"Was he in a relationship?

Hannah and Margaret looked at each other before turning their gaze back to the detectives.

"He was seeing Wendy."

"Wendy?"

"Wendy Griffiths."

"How was their relationship?" The DI's voice was soft.

Margaret's voice was breaking, as she answered. "It was up and down."

"I understand he telephoned you, the night he disappeared?"

"He was on his way home. He was missing Wendy, they'd had a row earlier that day."

"Could he have hurt himself because of that row?"

"No!" Hannah stood up. "He said he was going to make it up to her. He was missing her. He said he'd see her the next day and talk it through."

"And he gave no indication that he would want to hurt himself?"

"None."

"How did the conversation end?"

"He was cut off." Margaret reached out to grab the DI's arm, as though to emphasise this fact.

"Cut off?"

"Mid sentence. Like he was interrupted."

"Could that interruption have been due to his slipping and falling into the river?"

"No." Again Hannah was emphatic.

"Maybe." Margaret scratched her furrowed forehead.

"Did you hear a splash at all? Did you hear running water?"

"No, I...No I didn't. I really didn't."

Yvonne noted this in her pocketbook. "Can you remember what his last words were?"

"'I'm on my way.' He said, 'I'm on my way. I'm not sure where...'"

"He was on his way home and perhaps he felt lost?"

"I'm not sure, he didn't finish the sentence. It sounded like he was about to tell me where he was on his way to."

"But he didn't get to finish?"

"No."

"How did he sound? Did he sound drunk to you?"

"He was slurring his words-"

"*Mum.*" Hannah scowled at her mother. Then looked accusingly back at the detectives. "He wasn't so drunk he was going to go fall in the river. Lloyd has been drunk lots of times and has never even come close to falling in the river. There's a killer out there. Why don't you go and find him?" Hannah sat back, breathless.

Margaret broke down.

Yvonne knew better than to argue. In any event, her thoughts were leaning towards Hannah's. She was a long way from convinced that this was an accidental drowning.

"One last thing, and I'm sorry to ask this, Mrs Jones," Yvonne said in hushed tones, "did Lloyd ever use drugs?"

"No. No, he wouldn't." Mrs Jones looked up at the detective, her eyes earnest.

"I think you should leave now." Hannah's eyes flashed fire. "I thought you were supposed to help us, not make things worse."

"I'm going to do everything I can to help you, I promise." Yvonne's eyes were gentle, as she closed her notebook. "I know these questions can come across as cold. They're not meant to...it's sometimes an unfortunate consequence of trying to gather all the facts. But, if someone *did* murder your son and brother, I *will* find him, and I will bring him to justice."

Hannah's face softened and, as she led Dewi and Yvonne back to the door, she placed a hand on the DI's arm.

"Please," it was almost a whisper, "don't give up on my brother."

"I won't," the DI reassured with firm eye contact. "Is there anything else you want to tell me?"

Hannah looked back to where they had come, as though checking her mother was or wasn't there. "I think there was a row that night, at the Sportsman. One of my friends' partners witnessed it. It wasn't a fight or anything, but it got a bit heated."

"Who was the row between?"

"Lloyd and a local farmer."

"And the farmer's name, Hannah?"

"Clive. Clive Jones. He owns the farm out by Dingle Hall." Hannah proceeded to give the detectives directions, which they thanked her for, before making their way back to the car.

YVONNE DROVE MORE SLOWLY to the second house. She parked the car in Robin Square, part of the Maesyrhandir housing estate, to the south of Newtown centre. The houses were small, built for those workers brought in to fill the factories during the seventies and eighties. She turned off the engine and sat there for a minute or so.

"This is going to be even tougher than the last one." Dewi sighed, looking at his watch. "We could be some time."

Yvonne nodded, her silent gaze taken up by the young children of varying ages, playing football on the tarmac car park, using their shirts as goalposts. Happy. Carefree. Only a few short weeks ago, Callum would have been one of them.

A few of the neighbours were outside chatting over cups of tea, tinkering with cars or hanging out washing. She breathed deeply, readying for yet another heart-rending conversation with a grieving family. This time, that of Callum Jenkins. And, no matter what anyone said, this was definitely the hardest part of the job.

"You can stay here, if you like." She turned back to her DS.

"You deliver it better than I can." He sighed. "I feel like a coward."

She shook her head and gave her DS a sad smile. "Never."

Taking a large lungful of air, she stepped out into the hot, August afternoon.

HER HEART BEAT FASTER, as she waited for the door to open. She wiped clammy palms on her skirt, licking her lips to mitigate their sudden dryness. She felt as though she might struggle to speak.

When the door finally opened, Callum's stepfather filled it. He welcomed her inside, still wearing his work overalls. "I'd shake your hand, but..." He drew her gaze to his open hands, smeared with black oil. Smeared with hard work. To her left, she could see engine parts on the kitchen table. He'd clearly brought that work home with him.

"It's okay." She smiled, and felt a relief that he seemed more relaxed today. Sad, but calm.

"My wife is through there. I'm going to go get washed up." He nodded toward the living room door. She knew it was the living room, this being the second time she had visited.

The DI poked her head tentatively around the door.

Mrs Jenkins was sat holding a photograph album. It was clear she'd been crying, but had wiped the tears away with the hanky clutched in her right hand. She looked up expectantly as Yvonne entered. "Any news?"

Yvonne shook her head, the edges of her mouth curling downwards. "Not yet."

"This is my favourite photo of him." Sarah Jenkins turned the album around for the DI to take a look.

Yvonne leaned in close. Stunning. The blonde-haired boy, looking back at her, had an ethereal quality. Piercing blue eyes that, even from a photograph, appeared as though they might see *everything* inside of her. See through to her soul. His smile was haunting. The phrase 'not for this world' came unbidden to her mind. "Such a beautiful child, Mrs Jenkins."

"I hear him, sometimes." Mrs Jenkins closed the album. "I heard him last night. I heard his feet on the stairs."

Yvonne nodded.

"He doesn't want to leave, you see. It wasn't his time."

"Have you seen his father?"

Sarah shook her head. "He still can't bring himself to meet us. He's still angry at us...even now. He did speak to me by phone. He wasn't very nice. He still hasn't forgiven me for his not getting joint custody. Judge decided he drinks too much."

"I see."

"He wants to see you. Ask you about the investigation." Sarah sighed. "He wants to know what leads you have."

"I'll call him." Yvonne pursed her lips. "We've been making inquiries at the school. Trying to find all parents with light-coloured four-by-fours. Officers are going through the lists."

"You think it was another parent?"

The DI ran a hand through her hair. "It's a possibility we're considering. Plantation Lane is a twenty-mile-an-hour zone, with humps. The only people likely to be using it are residents, parents of the schoolchildren, and users of the sports centre. It's time-consuming work but we we'll get there. We'll have to interview everyone from those three groups who owns or drives a similar vehicle. Then, of course, there's rental and courtesy cars. We can't rule out a hire car, though we haven't found a garage, yet, that's repaired any damage. And, by now, a hire firm would likely have come forward if they had received a damaged car back from a client."

The sound of heavy footfalls on the stairs heralded the return of Callum's step-dad, Peter. Barefoot, and still drying his hair with a towel, he entered the room and took a seat opposite Yvonne.

The detective could see how tired he was. How tired they both were. She smoothed her skirt and moved forward, to perch on the edge of the sofa. "I'm afraid I'm going to have to go now, but, if you need anything, please call me. I'll call you if we discover anything." She pulled a wry smile. "Well, for anything I can safely disclose."

THE DARKNESS WAS thick enough to cut, there being no moon. He parked his car in a passing point, and waited. Engine off. Lights out. The wind broke the eerie silence, whistling in and around, rattling the car every now and then. He chewed his thumbnail, biting small pieces off it and chewing them in impatience.

At last he saw lights but did not turn his on - not until he was sure it was the man he was here to meet. It wouldn't do to have anyone else see him up here.

The other car parked up close behind, its lights shining right into his car. He grabbed a torch, got out and slammed his door *shut, striding to the other car. He shone his own light into the driver's eyes, knowing that he wouldn't be seen behind it.*

"Bloody hell, turn that thing off, will ya?" The other man put his hand in front of his face, to protect himself from the blinding light.

"You got what I want?" He took a quick scan around the deserted moors, near Dolfor, and satisfied himself there were no observers.

"I got your GBH."

"GHB." He found himself correcting, even though he knew GBH to be the street slang.

"Well, d'you want it or not?" The dealer was as impatient as he was. Little did he know he was on the hit-list. Not yet, though. He needed him. Needed what he could supply.

"Keep your hair on, Kenny," he barked. "Just give me the bag." He continued to hold the torch in the other man's face.

A scrabbling sound came from inside the car and a plastic bag was shoved through the window. He snatched at it with a gloved hand.

"What about my fucking money?" Kenny made to open his car door.

"Just be grateful I haven't told the cops what I know about you."

"You wouldn't. Where would you get your stuff?" Kenny scowled.

He bit his lip, tossing an envelope into Kenny's car, before turning his back and heading towards his own.

"Hey, I haven't counted it, yet."

"It's all there." He got quickly into his driver's seat and flicked on the engine. There was a thin screech as he pulled away. He headed back down towards Dolfor.

6

BREADCRUMBS

"So this is where he went in." Dewi leaned over to get a better look at the flattened grass and skid marks in the mud.

"His phone was found just there." Yvonne pointed to a place just beyond the top of the skid marks.

"Poor bugger." Dewi narrowed his eyes.

"Except, I don't believe he really went in here. His injuries don't fit." Yvonne moved over, to let Dewi get a better look at the bottom. "A fall down there would have resulted in severe bruising and probably broken bones."

Dewi pursed his lips and, taking hold of a tree branch as an anchor, made his way a little further down the bank, to one side of the marks.

"Careful, Dewi. We don't want you falling in there."

"You've got a point," he called back, shouting to be heard above the rushing water. "And SOCO didn't find blood anywhere on those rocks."

"Exactly."

"So where'd he go in? And why did his mobile phone end up here?" Dewi made his way back up, accepting the hand Yvonne held out to him. "Thanks." He brushed himself down.

"He was in the middle of a conversation with his mum when the phone went dead. Perhaps he fell, managed to get himself up, but dropped his phone, couldn't find it and wandered on."

"It's really steep down there. I don't think he would have been able to get back up from where those skid marks end. I went down as far as I could, any further and I would have been stuck, or fallen in, and I was not even at the bottom of those marks."

"Hmmm..." Yvonne scanned to her left and right, along both ways of the river path. "So, what was he doing here? He was supposed to be on his way home. Why does he take a route diametrically opposite to the way he's meant to go?"

"Maybe he wanted to go to the car park. There's a toilet there."

"But why not cut straight across Broad Street from the pub and walk down the cut-through? Why come so far along?"

"Perhaps he changed his mind and decided to pee in the river. That's when he lost his footing."

"Dewi, there are perfectly good toilets in the pub."

"So, what do *you* think happened?"

"I think he may have been meeting someone. Something bad happened and the scene was staged to mislead us."

"But, meeting who?"

"I don't know, Dewi, but I do know he was desperate to get back with his girlfriend, Wendy. Perhaps we should start by speaking to her. Even if she didn't speak to him that night, she may know more about his associates."

"Righty-oh."

"Also, get the guys onto the pub staff. There was an alter-

cation between Lloyd and a farmer. There's an outside
chance that Lloyd was going out of his way due to wanting
to avoid someone. Perhaps that someone was the farmer?
Ask them if he had any enemies."

"Will do."

"Also, can you find out how far they've got with checking
vehicles that may have killed the little boy. Tell them that
case is *still* priority."

Dewi headed off down the path, leaving the DI ponder-
ing. It was a good ten minutes before she headed off to
her car.

WENDY RENTED a two-bedroom home in Barnfields, only a
quarter of a mile from Lloyd's parents' home - as the crow
flies. Yvonne parked her car on the lane outside and
smoothed down her skirt.

There was no need to knock on the door. Wendy was
outside cleaning her silver Shogun. Wearing faded old jeans
and a sweatshirt, her blonde hair tied up in a pony tail, she
didn't hear the DI approach. She was lost in whatever music
was pouring through her headphones. Yvonne approached
with caution, worried she would make the girl jump.

She needn't have been concerned. Wendy pushed back
her headphones and stood, to survey her handiwork on the
car, lifting a watering can to wash off the suds.

"Wendy Stevens?" Yvonne took her opportunity.

Wendy swung round. "Yes?"

"Hello. I'm DI Giles, Dyfed-Powys police."

A dark cloud settled on Wendy's face, as though her
insides were sinking. "You've come about Lloyd." She put
down the watering can.

"Yes."

"Do you want to come inside?" Wendy pushed stray hair from her face with a wet hand.

"If that would be alright." Yvonne gave her a smile.

"Of course. I'll put these things away." Wendy led the way into her kitchen. Clean and well cared for, Wendy's home felt welcoming. A fresh vase of bright orange crocosmia set the room off beautifully. Putting down her tools, she washed and dried her hands, before putting the kettle on. "What happened to him?" She turned to face the detective, her back leaning against the countertop.

"He drowned. I'm so sorry.' Yvonne sat on a chair next to the kitchen table.

"Yes, but how? How could Lloyd fall in the river?"

"You weren't together, were you?" Yvonne asked, her voice low.

Wendy cast her eyes down. She kicked her heel into the cupboard behind her. "We've had our difficulties. I'd finished it a few times, only to go back. I often felt we'd be better as friends."

"What made you go back to him each time, if you felt it wasn't working?"

"I do care for him. Did. I *did* care for him. He would beg me to see him again and I always gave in."

"What were the main difficulties between you?"

"We wanted different things. He would want to go out, I would want to stay in. He was a good-time guy, I was the studious one. It's always been like that. We've known each other since primary school."

"I see."

"He wouldn't kill himself. He cared about me, but us breaking up would not have resulted in him tossing himself into the river. He just wasn't like that. Oh, he might be sad for a few weeks. Might have phoned me regularly to ask me back." Wendy bit her lip. "But he wouldn't have thrown himself in the river."

"Had he ever threatened to do anything like that?"

"No. Never."

"What do you think might have happened to him?"

"Me?" Wendy rubbed her forehead. "I think he either fell in or got into a fight and was pushed."

"Did he get into fights when he was out?"

"Not usually. I've only ever known him get into one, a few years back. He waded in when a friend was being threatened outside a nightclub."

"I see. Did he phone you that night?

"He did."

"What time was that?"

"I don't know, exactly, but it would have been around eight-thirty. I'd been expecting him to call."

"You'd already arranged it?"

"No. He just always called me when he was drinking, especially if we'd had a row or split up."

"What did he say?"

"He told me that he loved me and that he was sorry I felt let down by him."

"Had he let you down?"

"Not specifically, it just wasn't working. I wish…" Wendy gazed at the floor, eyes glazed. "I wish I'd spent longer talking to him. I wish I'd told him to come round. I really miss him."

"So, you didn't arrange to meet him anywhere?"

Wendy looked up, her eyes meeting those of the detective. "Meet him somewhere? No. I didn't arrange to meet him."

"And you're sure of that."

"Yes. You...you don't think I had something to do with this, do you?" Wendy's eyes were large and round.

"No." Yvonne shook her head. "I don't."

"Believe me, I've gone over and over whether I could have said or done something different."

Yvonne set down her notebook and gratefully took the offered mug of tea. "Look, you couldn't have known this would happen. No-one could."

"His family think he was murdered, don't they?"

"I think it's too early to speculate." Yvonne took a mouthful of tea. "Did he have any enemies?"

"None that I know of."

"Did he take illicit drugs?"

"No.' Wendy slapped her hand down on the counter-top. "He would *never* do drugs."

"Okay." The DI changed tack. "They said he'd had an argument with Clive Jones, a farmer, the night he disappeared. Were you aware of difficulties between them?"

Wendy shook her head.

"Is there anything else you'd like to tell me?"

Again, Wendy shook her head.

"All right." Yvonne closed her pocketbook. "Look, thank you for your time. I am really sorry for your loss."

Wendy nodded and gave a weak smile. "I hope you find out how this happened to him."

Yvonne rubbed her chin. "Me too.'

BACK AT THE STATION, Yvonne plopped a file down on her desk and downed the dregs of her tea. She leafed the file open. At the top of the pile, basic info and a photograph of James Owen.

The twenty-one-year-old had been pulled from the River

Severn nearly eight weeks ago. Like Lloyd, he'd been out drinking with friends and had left them, in the small hours, to walk home alone. Strong and athletic, his family had found it hard to believe he could just have fallen in the river and drowned. After his blood alcohol levels were disclosed, however, they had accepted it without further question, even though he had been only two-and-a-half times over the legal limit for driving.

"What you got?" Dewi perched on the corner of her desk.

The DI ran her hand through her hair and sighed. "James Owen's file. It says he'd been missing for three weeks, when he was found."

"I remember." Dewi rubbed the back of his neck. "He was found somewhere they'd already thoroughly searched... or so they thought."

Yvonne pursed her lips. "Maybe he was swept there from upstream. The river has been high and fast-flowing for weeks."

Dewi shook his head. "If I remember rightly, he was still submerged. So, he was likely found where he went in."

Yvonne flicked through a few pages. "You're right, Dewi. He was still fully submerged. Hmm. How long does it take for putrefaction gases to raise the body? A few days? A couple of weeks? This time of year the water's warmer. The body wouldn't stay submerged for that long, surely?"

Dewi shrugged. "Maybe we should ask Hanson for a guide. Are you thinking he didn't go into the water the same night he went missing?"

"I don't know, but you did say that the stretch of river he was found in had previously been thoroughly searched. Don't you think that's odd?"

"What does it say in the file?"

Yvonne leafed through more pages. "There was no sign of foul play. There's no detail in here about the search. Only about his being found. What about your frogman friend?"

"Carwyn?"

"Yeah. Would he be able to tell us why they didn't find him during the first search?"

"I can ask him what he thinks, I guess."

"Was he present during the search?"

"I would have thought he would have been. I'll talk to him."

"Please."

Yvonne returned to the file. A note had been placed in it to say that James had had an argument earlier that night with a barman. The altercation had happened in the Sportsman pub, before James left to go to the Castle Vaults - the last time he talked to anyone. He had then been seen on CCTV, staggering over the bridge at the top of town, before vanishing.

The barman's name was Geoff Griffiths. The DI decided she would speak to Geoff, as he would have been sober and someone who would be able to describe to her the demeanour of James and tell her whether James appeared drunk enough to simply fall in the river.

7

THE ROOM AT THE TOP OF THE HOUSE

The lad began to stumble, a look of confusion on his handsome features. His hunter couldn't make a move, yet. There was still a chance he'd be caught on CCTV. He took a dark, side alley down to where his van was parked and leaned on it to centre himself. As silently as he could, he opened the side door and waited.

As the boy rounded the corner, he could hear him talking on his mobile phone. He waited, his back to the back of the van. Controlling his breathing, so as not to be heard, he looked up at the black and white houses. No-one in the windows. He checked left and right, down the street.

The lad was unsteady on his feet, as he came within range. He took his chance, leaping out to place one hand over the mouth of his quarry, whilst the other hand grabbed the mobile phone. His thumb pressed the off button. The young man's defence was weak and uncoordinated. He was easily pulled into the side of the van. He was beginning to lose the ability to move.

~

"WHAT'S YOUR NAME, BOY?"

He was coming round, trying to open his eyes, which were glazed as though struggling to focus.

"What's your name?"

"Steve."

"Steve what?"

"Steve Bryant."

"Do you know where you are, Steve?" He gave a snort.

His captive began struggling against the bindings. He was naked from the waist up. The killer could see the lad's abdominal muscles straining, as he fought to free himself. The killer had anticipated this and put several layers of gauze beneath the ropes. He couldn't afford to leave marks.

"How old are you, Steve?"

"Nineteen. Who are you? I've seen you somewhere before. Why am I here?" Anger and fear cracked his voice.

The abductor blinked and cocked his head, signalling a cold curiosity. "I'm your killer."

The latter made the boy struggle all the more. He gave a sob, as he realised he was making no progress.

His would-be killer left the room.

Steve gazed around. The sloping roof told him this was an attic room, meaning he was at the top of a house. He tried to move the chair he was bound to, to look through the window, but found that the chair was bolted to the floor. His mouth was scratchy and his lips cracked. His muscles ached from being in the same position. He did his best to straighten up in an attempt to relieve the discomfort.

His vision having cleared, Steve was able to take in the room. Opposite, an open lap-top sat on a desk. He could see words on the screen that appeared to be moving upwards. On the right-hand-side, he was sure he could see himself on a chair in the room. The bastard was filming him.

*The rest of the room appeared old and rarely-used, there
being various items, from boxes to clothes to books that looked like
they hadn't been touched in years. Dust and cobwebs were everywhere. The only window was dirty and home to several spiders.
He hung his head.*

THE SPORTSMAN WAS QUIET. Just a couple of middle-aged
men propping up the bar, deep in conversation. Through
the archway, she could see three youngsters playing pool.
Other than that, the low-lying tables were as empty as the
fireplace. If there had been other imbibers here, they'd now
gone elsewhere - no doubt, to find lunch.

Yvonne sat on a stool at the end of the bar and waited,
taking the time to mull over the recent deaths. She didn't
have to wait long. Geoff Griffiths, the barman, returned with
a small box filled with packets of salted peanuts. He began
refilling the behind-the-bar stash. He looked almost too big
to work behind that tiny bar, she mused. He had to be at
least six-foot-four and, although not exactly overweight, he
looked well-built and muscular. She decided he must
work out.

He saw the DI waiting for him and called out, "Sarah?
Can you come and take over for a minute?"

A young woman, around eighteen, red-hair in a ponytail, came through from a back room. She gave Yvonne a
flushed, shy smile. "What can I get you?"

Yvonne held her hand up. "Nothing, thank you. I'm not
here for a drink. I came to speak to Mr Griffiths."

"Oh, I'm sorry." The girl coloured and shrank away.

The DI smiled. "It's okay."

"So, officer, how can I help you?" Geoff stared at her, unblinking. She found it unnerving and cleared her throat. "I wanted to discuss an altercation you might have witnessed the other night. Saturday the nineteenth of June, to be exact."

"What altercation? Can you be more specific?"

"We're conducting inquiries around the death of a young man you may have heard of. James Owen. His body was found in the river a couple of months back. Does that ring any bells?" She took out her pocketbook. "Did you know James Owen?"

"The first lad who was found in the river?"

"Yes."

He began polishing a glass. "I'd seen him around, yeah."

"In here?"

"Sometimes here, sometimes in the Castle. I often go for a drink myself, after I finish a shift."

"I see. Do you remember the argument here on the nineteenth of June? The one you helped split up?"

"Not sure-"

"I think you may have had words with James before he left. Some friends of his had stated that he wasn't happy with how he was dealt with."

"And this was the night he disappeared?"

"Yes. Saturday the nineteenth of June." She repeated the date slowly, emphasising each word, suspecting that he knew full-well what she was talking about. Death did that to people. It brought their memories into sharp focus. So, why not his?" She shifted on her seat. "Can you remember, now?"

"He was drunk. He was very drunk and slurring his words."

"I see." Yvonne rubbed her chin. "I'm a bit confused over that. You see, at least two of his friends described him as being only a bit tipsy, whilst he was here. They stated that he only became *drunk* later on at The Castle. But, that's not how you remember it?"

He looked at her as though she had two heads, his lip curling up at one side. "Well, they might have found it hard to judge, their being drunk, themselves. I was stone-cold sober." He sneered the last sentence.

Her eyes narrowed. "What was the argument about?"

"Oh, I think one of the other lads had made a comment about his girlfriend being too good for him."

"Can you remember who that other lad was?"

"Rob? I think his name was Rob Davies."

"How did James respond?"

"He was angry. Looked like he wanted to hit Rob. I stepped out from behind the bar. There was a little bit of shoving going on and I didn't want a full-on fight breaking out in here."

"So you intervened?"

"I came out and I told them to cool it. Told them if they wanted to have a go at each other, to take it outside."

"And did they?"

"No. They just glowered at each other and brushed themselves down. Friends moved in between them, then."

"So, how did you become involved in an exchange with James?"

"A third of his drink had spilled in the argument. He thought it was when I got involved and pushed them away from each other."

"Did he shout at you?"

"He demanded that I replace the drink."

"Demanded or asked?" Yvonne wanted to be sure.

"Demanded. I told him, at first, that he'd have to pay for it and he refused."

"So, what happened?"

"I told him I'd get him another drink, but then I wanted him to leave the bar and go cool off."

"And did he?"

"Not straight away. I gave him a fresh pint and he took his time drinking it. Still upset, I guess. He went outside to make a phone call shortly afterward and then I think he went to the Castle. I saw him, just briefly, when I went there for a pint."

"Would you say he was falling over drunk, when you saw him?"

"Yeah. I would. I know it's sad and all, but I wasn't surprised to hear he'd fallen in the river. He was a disaster waiting to happen. I think he was always getting jealous over his girlfriend's friendships with other men."

Yvonne's eyes shot up from her notebook to his face. "How would you know that?"

"I'm a barman, I hear a lot of things. Anyway, it was mentioned, more than once, during the argument he had with Rob. I should think everyone who was here became aware."

The DI fell silent. She thought of James. Had he felt that everyone was either laughing at him or judging him? Is that what had made him lash out? The things she had been learning about him didn't really tally with someone who went looking for fights.

"Do you know how I can get hold of Rob Davies?" She tapped her pen on her book.

"Sure. He's studying at Newtown College."

"Coleg Powys?"

"Yeah."

"Thanks for your time." Yvonne eased herself off the barstool, pulling her skirt over her knees when Geoff Griffith's eyes strayed to them. She thought she heard him snigger.

8

NEW RECRUITS

Morning briefing was quieter than normal. Several officers had gone down with Norovirus and would be off for the week. Yvonne counted herself lucky that she and her sergeant had so far managed to avoid the sickness which was also ravaging the schools in the area.

Two very young-looking officers stood next to DCI Llewellyn, who waited for the rest of them to quiet down and pay attention. Both were dark-haired. The small-framed female nervously chewed on a fingernail and the tall male shifted his weight every few seconds. Yvonne felt sorry for them having to stand up at the front. She gave them both a smile and a nod.

The DCI emphasised clearing his throat. "Okay, I know we're thin on the ground this week, but we have a job to do, and the sooner I get started, the sooner you can get on. I'd like to introduce you to two probationers, both on a fast-track scheme: PCs Chris Halliwell and Jenny Hadley."

Greetings from the floor ensued before the DCI continued.

"They're going to be with us on secondment for a couple of months, to get a feel for what it is we do here in CID. Make them welcome and be prepared to answer lots of questions. They won't learn without asking. Obviously, I'm not expecting you to share anything that's especially sensitive in an ongoing investigation but, otherwise, treat them as a part of the team. Any questions?"

A few were fired at the DCI. They made Yvonne feel uncomfortable. She was always surprised by some officers' reluctance to mentor new recruits. She understood that it took time out of busy schedules to explain processes and procedures, but everyone had to start somewhere and, in her experience, fresh eyes and keen minds were always a bonus. She looked forward to working with trainees.

As it turned out, one of them was assigned to her.

"DI Yvonne Giles." She smiled and extended her hand.

"Chris Halliwell." He smiled back, his handshake a little damp.

"Where've you come from, Chris? Come on, Dewi's making us a brew. I'll introduce you to the rest of my team."

"I'm from Shrewsbury, ma'am."

"Aha, just over the border."

"Born and bred."

"So, what brings you to Wales?"

"Honestly?"

She grinned. "*Obviously*."

"Placements around the whole of the UK are pretty tight. Dyfed-Powys offered me a place."

"I see." Yvonne indicated the direction to the coffee area. "Well, I promise you won't regret it."

"It *is* beautiful, here," he concurred.

"Just in time." Dewi was finishing making drinks for himself, the DI, Chris Halliwell and DC Jones. DC Clayton was absent, being one of the officers who had gone down with Norovirus.

"This is DC Callum Jones, and DS Dewi Hughes." Yvonne nodded in Dewi's direction. "DS Hughes makes the best tea in the station."

Dewi grinned. "I can't quite remember what Yvonne's tea tastes like-"

Yvonne laughed. "The cheek of it! Why, I'm sure I made one only the other day."

"Exactly." Dewi put his hands on his hips in mock indignation.

Chris laughed with everyone else and the DI was happy he seemed more relaxed.

"I'm pleased to meet you all," he said, shaking hands with the two men. "Can I ask what sort of cases you're working on?"

Yvonne nodded. "We've got a few things on the go, but the most pressing are a hit-and-run death of a young boy and three river deaths. On the face of it, the river deaths look like accidental drownings, but I think there are a few loose ends that need exploring, including their close proximity in time." She grimaced. "Though, I'm not sure everyone agrees with me about that."

"No, I can see where you're coming from." Dewi handed round the mugs. "I don't think we'd be doing the families justice if we didn't investigate any doubts - no matter how small."

"How old are you, Chris? If you don't mind my asking?" Yvonne tilted her head to one side.

"Twenty-two, ma'am." He took a sip of his tea and nodded appreciatively towards Dewi.

"Then, you're not much older than the three young men we found floating in the river after they'd been out on the town."

PC Halliwell cleared his throat. "I see."

Yvonne patted him on the back. "Anyway, we'll look a little more at these cases, shortly. For now, let's drink up and I'll show you around.

THE FOLLOWING DAY, Yvonne strode into the station an hour earlier than usual. Dewi was waiting for her.

"Dewi? I got your message. What was so urgent?" The DI stood catching her breath.

"Sorry, ma'am. I didn't have time to leave a longer voice-mail. They found another body in the river this morning. No identification, as yet. I've been looking through missing persons and there's a couple of possibilities. I think it most likely to be a Steven Bryant, a nineteen-year-old college student. He was studying law at Aberystwyth University, and staying with his parents, in Newtown, for the summer. Missing for three weeks...er," Dewi checked his notes, "went missing on a Saturday."

"Saturday day-time?"

"Early hours of Saturday, ma'am."

"Oh no...when did you know he was missing?"

"Only now. I got a call from Callum. He'd been working with uniform on a drugs bust, in the small hours, when news of the body came in. I got here as soon as I could. I've been checking MisPer lists."

"How come we didn't know sooner?"

"I've taken a look on the system. We were only informed six days ago, ma'am, it seems there was some confusion, as the family thought he may have gone back to Aberystwyth to stay with friends. It was something he'd mentioned doing. It's only when he'd been away for a couple of weeks, and they had had no contact in that time, that they began to be concerned. Apparently it wasn't unusual for him to just take off, sometimes."

"What is going on?" The DI ran a hand through her hair and stared through the window, deep lines furrowing her forehead. "Three young men dead in the river in such a short time frame..." She shook her head. "Let me know as soon as his identity is confirmed, okay?"

Dewi sighed, and, as she turned back towards him, the DI noticed he was looking a little dishevelled.

"Is everything alright, Dewi?"

"Fine, ma'am. Why d'you ask?"

"You're looking tired."

"Oh." Dewi gave a chuckle. "We had our eighteen-month-old grandson to stay last night. Gave us the runaround. I'll sleep like a log tonight." Dewi nodded over in the direction of someone bent over a PC in the corner.

Yvonne raised her eyebrows and whispered, "Halliwell? What's he doing here so early?"

"Obviously an early bird." Dewi shrugged.

PC Halliwell looked up from his notes.

Yvonne nodded at him, turning back to Dewi. "Are they still at the river?"

"Ma'am?"

"The recovery. Is it still in progress? Or has it finished?"

"It's still in progress, as far as I know. I thought you might like to go down there."

"You're right, I would." The DI grabbed a spare pen and shouted to PC Halliwell for him to follow them.

THE RIVER LEVEL had dropped several inches, though it was still fast flowing. The body was barely forty feet from the bridge in Newtown, known as The Long Bridge. It looked like it had been caught by a large branch, at the edge of rapids. The DI could see that the stomach of the dead man was severely bloated. He lay face up. The police photographer stood in the river, needing every inch of his waste-high waders. He took a number of shots prior to the body being loaded onto the rescue dinghy.

Yvonne left the river path and took a narrow, dirt cut-through to a stony beach by the water. Chris Halliwell followed. Dewi was deep in conversation with his friend, Carwyn.

The DI stood, hands deep in her jacket pockets. Watching. Thinking. A brisk breeze teased out tendrils of her hair and busied them round her face. She brushed them away distractedly, only for them to return. The sounds from the busy main road above disappeared as she stared across the water, trying to picture the victim's last moments. The suspicions she had toyed with previously were fermenting into something which felt urgent to her. Two bodies were too many, and now there were three. If this became four, she would hold herself personally responsible.

Halliwell stood silently beside her, observing and respecting her silence. He was a good foot-and-a-half taller. He crouched, leaning his arm on his knees.

"Do you have a family?" Yvonne asked, still looking ahead of her to the activity on the river.

His eyes widened, as though taken aback by the question. "I...I have a mum and a daughter, who I don't see anywhere near as often as I'd like to."

"A daughter?" Yvonne looked at him properly now. He didn't look old enough. She said so.

"I won't say it was a mistake." Halliwell shook his head. "I could never see her as a mistake. But she was the result of a one-night-stand, when I was seventeen. She's nearly six. She's hemiplegic. Bright as a button, but the right side of her body doesn't work as well as her left. I idolise her."

Yvonne gave him a wistful smile. "What's your daughter's name?"

"Sally."

"Lovely name."

"Thank you."

"So, how come you don't see her as often as you'd like?"

"I work shifts and her mum is married to a guy who isn't exactly a fan."

"I see-"

"But the light in my little girls eyes...when she sees me." He shook his head again. "It's like nothing else. To see her push her weaker leg as fast as she can, to run into my arms. It's all I can do to hold back the tears."

Yvonne nodded, a soft smile curling the corners of her mouth. She held out a hand and rubbed his arm.

Dewi made his way over.

"Who found him, Dewi?" Yvonne put her hands back in her pockets.

"A dog walker saw what they thought was a large bag floating in the river. The dog ran towards it, barking, apparently. It was then that the owner took a closer look and realised it was actually a body."

"How long has he been in the river?"

Carwyn seems to think at least a couple of weeks. Body is very gassy and the SAR guys are worried they might have de-gloving, if they're not very careful."

Yvonne shuddered. De-gloving referred to the skin coming away from the hands at the wrists, something which could happen if the body had been submerged long enough. She explained this to Halliwell.

"When will we know if it's Steven Bryant?" she asked Dewi.

"Later tonight, ma'am. DC Jones contacted the family, and Steven's father will be attending the mortuary this evening."

"I don't envy Carwyn his job, Dewi." The DI sighed.

Dewi shook his head. "Me neither, but we see our own fair share of death."

The DI couldn't argue with that.

YVONNE KICKED off her shoes and wandered through to her kitchen to pour an ample glass of South African chardonnay. A chicken curry slow-cooking in the oven, she carried the wine through to the dining table, where she had strewn as many photographs of the dead young men as she possessed.

Some of the photographs were those taken whilst they were still in the water, others were stills from CCTV, documenting a mere few minutes from their final hours. Yet others, were those taken in life and supplied by their families. Those were the photographs of the men in full bloom - smiling or laughing into the camera as they completed some dare-devil feat, or else relaxing with friends. Enjoying life. The DI sighed.

Looking at them in this way, she was struck by their similar appearance. She considered them all handsome. They were athletic and wiry. Similar height and weight, and a similar confidence in their eyes. From the information she had in front of her, they were all involved in sport of one form or another, and all had continued their education beyond school.

She was struck, also, by the similarity in the circumstances of their disappearance. All had been out with friends past midnight. All had become separated from those friends. All had set off home, alone. Young men drowning on their way home from a night out was becoming a *thing*. The question was, why?

She had consumed a good half of the wine before the phone call came in from Dewi. He had volunteered to be at the morgue when the latest victim's father arrived to identify him.

"Was it Steve, Dewi?" She held her breath.

"It was, ma'am."

"Oh god."

"Ted Bryant is going to come into the station again tomorrow. Apparently his son tried to text them the night he went missing. Nothing came through on the text."

"It was blank?"

"Yes. Nothing in it."

"Can you do that? Send a blank text?"

"Apparently, they tried calling him back but they just kept getting voicemail. They left several messages."

"Did SAR recover the phone?"

"No. His phone, jacket and wallet are missing."

"Maybe we're looking at a mugging gone wrong-"

"Could be, but he could have lost his jacket during his struggle to survive in the water. If the phone and wallet were in his jacket pockets, stands to reason they would be gone as well."

"Could you have a word with Carwyn? See if they'll check that stretch of river for the jacket?"

"I think they are already on it, but I'll check, ma'am."

"Thanks, Dewi. Now, get yourself home and don't rush in tomorrow, okay? I'll get Jones and Clayton to grab all the CCTV footage they can find, from the night he went missing. We'll go through it tomorrow afternoon."

"Right you are."

THEY WAITED WITH BAITED BREATH. DC Callum Jones fiddled with the file and finally got it working. "Okay, this is a compilation of all of the footage we've been able to get. We have five pieces altogether. We have video from three of the town cameras, footage from inside of the Castle vaults, and footage from the alleyway outside of the Castle Vaults. One of the town cameras caught him as he walked over the bridge on his way home. We lose him completely after that."

The images were grainy, but clear enough to understand what was going on. The initial footage showed Steven leaving the Sportsman with his friends and waving to them, as they walked on towards the Castle, and he went around the corner from the Sportsman, to Barclays, where he appeared to extract money from the auto-bank.

The footage then showed him walking the two hundred yards, along Broad Street, to the Castle. It struck Yvonne that, at that point, he was walking reasonably well and showed little sign of being so intoxicated he could fall into the river. She made a note.

The next footage was from inside of the Castle. It showed Steven at the bar, ordering a pint and then having various short conversations with friends and people he had just bumped into. It was obvious he knew them. He played one game of pool, which he narrowly lost, and then he said his goodbyes. He exited through the back door, into the alleyway.

At that point, the camera footage switched to that from the alley camera. Yvonne sat forward in her seat, peering at the screen. She could hardly credit that this was the same man. And yet, from his clothing and appearance, it was. But, this man wobbled. He almost stumbled down the steps. As he entered the alleyway, he set off one way, swayed, corrected himself, and then turned back the other way towards Broad Street.

He continued to sway as he fumbled for his mobile phone. He appeared to be having difficulty using it and, the DI suspected, this may have been when he tried texting his parents and sent the blank message.

"There." DC Clayton got up and paused the footage. "He's clearly had a skinful. Look at him with the phone, he's wobbling all over the place."

Yvonne pursed her lips. "I agree. But how?"

"Ma'am?"

"Well, you saw him leave the Sportsman. He got his money and walked up Broad Street. I didn't see him wobbling then."

"Right." Dewi nodded. "And we only see him having one pint after that. Are we really to believe that that one pint made such a difference?"

"We should find out when he ate. Could be that his stomach had only just emptied and a lot of alcohol hit his bloodstream at once."

Yvonne shook her head. "I know what you're saying, but I don't see it making that big a difference. Can we double-check the time frame. Have we got all the connecting footage?"

Callum did a rewind, confirming, for everyone, that they did indeed have everything and there were no gaps.

"He went to the toilet." Dewi tapped his pen on his chin. "Maybe he took something."

"That's what I was wondering." Yvonne stood up. "Except, I don't think he was known to use drugs. Anything on his parents' radar?"

Dai Clayton shook his head. "No history, and not suspected to be using by his family, or the friends questioned so far."

PC Halliwell cleared his throat. "Can we go back and watch his drink? Is it possible something was slipped into it by someone else? We know that his jacket, wallet and phone are still missing. Perhaps his drink was spiked to enable someone to take his stuff."

"Absolutely." Yvonne nodded vigorously. "I was thinking along the same lines. That was a massive change in his demeanour and it happened within about thirty minutes. I agree with Chris. I think there's a possibility his drink was tampered with."

The footage was rewound, but no tampering had been caught on camera. Unfortunately, only meagre glimpses of the pint were gleaned, as it sat on the edge of the bar. The Castle was packed and bodies continually moved back and for, obscuring their view.

"Well," Yvonne moved to the front of the room, to face them all directly. "At least we've got an idea of the condition he was in when he sent his parents the blank text. Callum, can you confirm with them the time?"

"Yes, ma'am."

"We also know that, in principle, he was intoxicated enough to be staggering, and therefore potentially liable to fall in the water, when wandering by the river."

There were nods and grunts from the rest of the team.

"But I have massive doubts around the reasons for his

intoxication and I can't get my head around how he ended up by the river, when we have footage of him staggering over Longbridge on his way towards the Cresent. He would have had to double-back on himself and descend the steep steps down to the river path. Which we know he didn't do, or we'd have it on CCTV."

"Unless he kept on going," Dewi offered. "He may have carried on past his parents' road and taken the bridge by MacDonalds. If he entered that car park, he could have accessed the river path there."

"Can we get the CCTV?"

"Will do, ma'am, but the coverage is not as good. We should have him if he is on that bridge, though, or if he entered or passed MacDonalds."

"Great. Keep on trying to trace his jacket and belongings, as well."

"Will do."

9

HIT AND RUN

"Dai, can I have a word?" Yvonne jogged after DC Clayton, as he fast-paced down the corridor. "Ma'am?"

"Any news on the small car involved in the hit-and-run? I said I'd call the parents later with any updates."

"Did I hear you say hit-and-run and updates, in the same sentence?" DCI LLewellyn approached from behind them.

Yvonne closed her eyes. "You did, sir, yes."

"Oh, good. So, are there any?" He placed both hands on his hips.

Dai Clayton grimaced. "Er, no."

"Can I ask why not? It's been four weeks."

Yvonne rubbed her chin.

Dai took out his pocketbook. "We've eliminated huge numbers of vehicles. Mostly those of parents of the school children, Garthowen and Maesyrhandir residents, and regular sports centre users. We've cross-checked vehicle regs from CCTV footage of Maldwyn sports centre car park and checked out those vehicles. None damaged and none had been to garages for damage-related work." Clayton sighed. "What we haven't been able to do is check out any through-traffic."

Yvonne nodded. "It's used as a cut-through, isn't it? When New Road is busy? Which it was, there having been a load shed from an artic lorry, down by the bridge at Nantoer. You can bet a couple of hundred vehicles went past the school that wouldn't normally have done so."

"Right." Clayton nodded. "And that's where we're at. We're working through the vehicle regs of the traffic which passed the camera near LIDL's store. It's time-consuming but we *will* get there." He directed the last at the DCI, accompanied by an unusually stern look.

The DCI cleared his throat. "Alright. Yvonne, keep me informed."

"I will, sir." Yvonne winked at Clayton.

After the DCI had continued down the corridor, the DI continued, "I've got to telephone the parents again, later today. I'll let them know how far we've got. Keep plugging away, Dai. I know it's back-breaking work, but that little boy deserves justice if anyone does."

Dai Clayton took in her soulful eyes. "It feels personal, doesn't it?"

"Incredibly so. He was at the start of his life, Dai. He had so much to look forward to. Some bastard took that away from him and did not have the guts to own up or to confront what they'd done. To say sorry to his family and friends. Too damn right, it's personal. Look, do you need more resources? I can put PC Halliwell at your disposal and-"

"I'll bear that in mind, thank you. I'm actually just off to see the tech bods to get their help on speeding the whole process up. They've got a few tricks and programs up their sleeve." He tapped Yvonne on the elbow. "We'll solve this. We'll bring this toe-rag to justice."

Yvonne smiled. "Thank you, Dai."

HE SIGHED for the umpteenth time. Why was that idiot Kenny always late. The whole world didn't run on Kenny-time. He kicked at a wheel on his car, just as a dust-cloud started up on the horizon. That'd be him, driving like the clown he was. He hawked at phlegm in the back of his throat, spitting it out on the grass, his face clouded in disgust. This was the part of his fantasy he could do without, but he couldn't enjoy the chase without it. He took a good look around the moor, the barren wilderness of it. It had a wild, bare beauty. He liked the sheep-gnawed rawness of it. A moon landscape. In the distance, modern-day windmills - some busy, some as still as pictures - broke up the horizon. No dwellings for as far as the eye could see.

"You alright, dude? How's it going?" Kenny drew up in his battered truck, window down and music up.

He wanted to push back the lank, unkempt hair from Kenny's face. The fact it hung everywhere irritated him beyond measure. "You're late. Where the hell have you been?"

"Hey, take a chill pill. I got here as soon as I could." Kenny leaned right back in his seat. "I'm a busy man. You gotta wait your turn-"

His arm shot through the open window. He turned off the thudding music before grabbing Kenny by the shirt collar. "Listen here, you greasy piece of shit. If you tell me you're going to be in a certain place at a certain time, you better-the-hell be there. I'm not one of your kids. You do not mess with me. Not if you value your life." He pulled Kenny's shocked face right up to his, and, baring his teeth, growled, "Am I making myself clear?" He let go, and Kenny dropped back.

"Crystal." Kenny readjusted his clothes. "I got held up at the roadworks, okay?"

"You got what I want?"

"Yeah. 'Course." Kenny reached into his glove compartment. "It'll cost ya a bit more this time."

"What do you mean, it'll cost more? Why?"

"Prices have gone up a bit at the mo. I...I'm not kidding, honest. There was a big bust, up in Manchester. Fuzz all over everything. It's left a hole in supply. We can still get it, it's just a little harder right now."

"There's always a problem, isn't there, Kenny?"

"Well, do you want it or not?" Kenny was attempting nonchalance but his voice trembled.

He pulled out an envelope, and counted through its contents. "How much more?"

"Fifty?" Kenny didn't sound too sure.

"I'll give you an extra twenty," he said, pulling out his wallet. "Think yourself lucky."

"But-"

"Fuck off outta here, Kenny." He threw the twenty-pound note through the open window.

Kenny glared at him, but shut his window and backed up, spinning into a fast u-turn. He disappeared the way he had come, dust clouds kicking up the horizon.

10

TORTURE

"So your name's William?" His hooded tormentor grunted, scraping a wooden chair along the floorboards as he positioned it just in front of him. "I think I'll call you Billy. I like that better."

Gagged, William could only mutter in return, pulling against his restraints in a vain attempt to free himself. He looked down the length of his body. He was laid out on some sort of trolley, covered in a cream blanket full of intended holes, like a hospital blanket. Over the top of that were wide-band leather straps. He couldn't exactly see how many, but there had to be at least five. All buckled in the middle.

"What do you think?" His captor smiled, and it was pure evil. "This way there'll be no marks."

He tried desperately to say something. His captor eased out of the chair, taking his time to walk over and remove the gag.

"What do you want from me? Let me go. Please. Let me go. What have I done to deserve this? Why am I here?"

His captor returned to his seat. "Nothing. You've done nothing. I'm not doing it because I think you deserve it. I'm doing this *because I get pleasure from it. So do they."* He flicked his head in the direction of the open laptop.

"Who's they?" William craned his head in an attempt to better see the laptop.

"My friends from the dark web. We all have the same need to watch people drown."

"You're sick."

"That depends on your perspective. Anyway, don't say that. You might upset them." He whispered the last, again nodding towards the laptop.

"Are people watching this?" William shook his head, incredulous. "Let me the fuck out of this crap."

"Don't get nasty. It'll just get worse for you if you get nasty."

William closed his eyes. Any moment now he was going to wake up. This was a nightmare. He'd had several pints too many and anytime now he was going to wake up with a hangover and laugh at all of this.

"You're wondering how you got here, aren't you?" His captor leaned back in the chair, legs out in front of him and crossed at the ankles.

"How did I get here?"

"I drugged you. It was easy. You leave your drinks all over the place. They all do."

"All? You mean there's more? You've done this to others?"

"A few."

"Oh my god."

"Yeah."

"What happens now?" There was a dawning on William's face. A sudden realisation that this was not the goal. He wasn't simply to be held bound and gagged in this room. His face ashen, he pulled again against his restraints, his eyes darting around the room. Terrified of what he might see and yet needing to know.

The chair scraped some more, as the tormentor got up once

more. From somewhere near the bottom of the trolley, the tormentor pulled out two large watering cans. They were full, evidenced by the difficulty he had carrying them.

Confusion clouded William's face. "What the-?"

His captor pulled out a hood, made from sack-material, from a cupboard drawer and paused to type something into the laptop. He appeared to wait for a reply and chuckled to himself. He then made his way to the side of the trolley.

"No...No, don't put that on me. Please don't put that thing on me!" The latter request turned into a shriek, as his captor forced the hood over his head, whilst William shook his head. The only way he could resist.

But the hood was on and William fell silent, breathing ragged. There were no holes for his eyes. He could see nothing, save the material of the hood.

His captor was pumping something with his foot. Part of the trolley, where his head and shoulders rested, lowered. His torso and legs were now higher than his head.

"Stop! Stop!" He began to splutter and choke, scrabbling for breath, as water was poured over his mouth and nose, through the hood. His words became a warbled noise, as he shook his head vigorously in a vain attempt to avoid the water going into his nose and mouth. He couldn't breath. He was sure he was going to drown. He screamed and warbled and blew out at the water.

Just when it felt like he might pass out, his tormentor stopped and placed the watering can back on the floor.

William gasped for breath, relieved he was still conscious.

"Had enough, Billy?"

"Yes." Billy sobbed.

He heard fingers on keys. The bastard was back on the laptop.

He lay as still as he was able, straining to hear what was happening. Unable to see where his tormentor was.

Again, a warbled cry, as yet more water began to pour on his face, robbing him of his breath and convincing him he was going to die. His chest and stomach were painful and he was sure he could feel water in his lungs. He didn't know how much more he could take.

Again, his captor stopped and pulled back the hood. "Had enough, Billy?"

"Fuck you!" William blurted out, between gulps of air, his spirit strengthened by anger. "What have I done to you?"

"I told you. You've done nothing. This isn't about you. It's about us."

William sobbed again. He was going to die. He knew it now. Was as certain of it as he had ever been of anything. This evil man wasn't going to stop. He'd done this before. He'd killed before and he was killing again. As the torture restarted, William lost consciousness.

GETTING the body to the river was no problem. After dressing the dead man in his clothes, and satisfying himself there was little in the way of obvious marks, the killer pulled a sack over the body and tied it to a sack-truck, to get it down the stairs. Secluded as he was, he had no fear of being seen as he got the body into his boot. It was all just a little too easy.

The body would stay there until nightfall. Then came the risky part - getting it to the river unnoticed. He'd planned for it, but there was still no telling who might be about. The spot he had chosen was just outside of town. Near enough that it would be seen as accidental drowning, but far enough to minimise any risk of being caught. All he had to do was wait.

11

A FRIEND IN NEED

Tasha had kicked her shoes off under the table at their favourite cafe, Bank Cottage, enjoying an Americano, when Yvonne arrived out of breath.

"Sorry I'm late." Yvonne placed her bag on the seat next to her and pulled a face, her head tilted to one side.

"Don't worry about it." Tasha grinned. "I'll go order you a Latte. Didn't get one straight away, as I wasn't sure if you'd be able to make it."

Yvonne placed her jacket on the back of her chair. "Oh, thank you. That's so thoughtful. You're right, we are ridiculously busy right now."

The DI sank into a chair and calmed. There was something about the old-world atmosphere in the little cafe that melted everything else away. Even, time itself.

"It'll be with us in a moment." Tasha was back, with that big, white, toothy smile.

"How's the house coming along? Sorry I haven't been up in a while." Yvonne extracted her phone from her bag and set it on the table beside her.

"Busy, then?" Tasha nodded towards the phone.

"I'm sorry." Yvonne sighed. "Yes. Yes, we're treading water at the moment."

"I tell you what. I'll tell you about the house *after* you tell me what you're working on."

Yvonne chuckled. "Okay. Fair enough."

The DI began by relating the hit-and-run to her friend, and talking of the team's frustration at the slow progress. Tasha listened, allowing her friend to release the tension and get it all out. Commiserating with her that the victim was so young, and his loss so needless.

"There's something else…" Tasha's eyes searched her face.

Yvonne looked down into her coffee.

"There is, actually. At least, I believe there is."

Tasha chuckled. "Uh-oh, here we go." She put the back of her hand to her forehead, in mock despair, before winking at the DI.

"I think I may be chasing another serial killer. Except, if I am, I'm not clear about motive."

"Go on…" Tasha leaned in close, her unblinking eyes narrowed.

"We've had three young men turn up in the river, in about the same number of months. All had been on nights out with their friends, prior to disappearing. All were supposedly on their way home at the time we think they disappeared. They ended up dead in the river."

"That's a short period of time for three bodies to turn up in the same stretch of river."

"Yes, it is. Not only that, but at least one of them was nowhere near the river when he was last captured on CCTV. He was only a few streets away from his home. He also appeared to become intoxicated in an extremely short period of time. All of them were young - twenty years old, give-or-take."

"I see."

"Thing is, as far as we can tell, there had been no sexual interference with the men, and there appeared to be no signs of violence, other than the kinds of damage expected in a case of drowning."

"So, your superiors think that the men fell in, whilst intoxicated, and drowned, and you have a feeling in your gut that tells you otherwise."

"That's pretty-much it, yes."

"Okay."

"In one of the cases, I suspect that the victim's phone was placed on the river bank to mislead us as to where the victim supposedly fell into the water."

"And you don't think he entered there."

"No. There were large rocks where he would have fallen and his injuries were not consistent with hitting those rocks from a height."

"I see."

"Although the most recent victim appeared to have lost his jacket, phone and wallet, the other victims still had either their phone or their wallet, and that makes robbery an unlikely motive."

"*If* it's the same killer."

"Right. *If* it's the same killer. But, we'd be damned unlucky if we had three different killers preying on young men on nights out."

"Absolutely. Okay, just supposing you have a killer. Just one killer for all three men. You know how his victims are being chosen, as they are all on nights out. They're intoxicated, therefore easier to control."

"What about motive? Any ideas?"

"Have you heard of people who get sexual gratification from the act of drowning someone? They can take a person almost to the point of death and then revive them. Rinse and repeat. Total control over the life and death of that person is what gives them pleasure. They can play god. Ultimately, they will kill their victim, as otherwise they risk discovery. Although, killing the person can, in any event, be the ultimate aim."

"But surely, death comes more swiftly to someone who's intoxicated."

"Perhaps, but there's no saying that once the killer has the person under control, he can revive them, even sober them up. If they're bound, he can still drown them."

Yvonne shook her head. "There's no evidence that any of the victims were bound."

"Sure, but a bright killer can find ways of binding, without necessarily leaving marks. Anyway, it's possible to bring someone under control with drugs. The mind knows what's happening but the body can do little about it."

Yvonne sat forward in her chair. "You know, I was wondering about that. The most recent victim appeared to go from fine to legless by drinking one extra pint, prior to his disappearance. I've been wondering if he could have been drugged with something like GHB. We checked CCTV but couldn't see the lad's pint for more than about a minute of the footage. He was playing pool for around fifteen minutes and his pint was up on the corner of the bar, but people were continually in the line of sight to it."

"Fifteen minutes is plenty of time for something to be slipped into his drink."

"Right. But that's all I've got. There's nothing all that concrete to go on and I could be barking up the wrong tree."

"Want me to come up with a profile?"

"Could you?"

"If you let me see relevant information from the case files, sure."

"I'll speak to the DCI. See if he'll let you do it officially. At least then you'll get paid. Otherwise-"

"It's okay. By all means, see if they'll pay me for it, but I'll do it for you, anyway. I'm in between cases for the Met. I can afford the time. Anyway, you've peaked my interest, DI Giles." Tasha grinned.

"Wow, this coffee's so good." Yvonne smiled. "Now, tell me how your house-by-the-sea is coming along."

Yvonne held her breath and wrung her hands, as she waited with Dewi on the riverbank.

Dewi shook his head. "I've never known anything like this. This has just never happened before. So many bodies in so short a time."

"These are no accidents, Dewi. We have a killer, right here on our patch. A killer who is picking off our young men. I know it." She strained to watch the divers, as they recovered the body from the pool. An underwater photographer had taken pictures for the coroner. They'd pulled out so many bodies now, the police authority had coughed up for the expensive piece of kit. The red dinghies were an all-too-familiar sight. The DI felt like crying.

"We've got a crazy in town." Dewi stared out across the water, eyes narrowed, like he was trying to figure it all out.

Carwyn Davies climbed out of the water, as the body and the dinghy were brought in for the waiting ambulance."This one's not right," he shouted to them.

Yvonne ran to meet him. "What do you mean, not right?"

"His eyes. They're not wide and glassy. Also, his head was tilted to one side."

"Meaning?" Yvonne pushed back her hair, resisting the urge to shout, 'Spit it out, man.'

"He didn't die in the water. Not in this water. He died somewhere else, on land. I believe he was placed in the water after death."

"You sure?" The DI frowned.

"We took photographs. They'll go to the coroner. This one will get a full post-mortem. I've a feeling Hanson will be confirming this as a murder enquiry." Carwyn pulled back his wet-suit hood, rubbing at the indented ring it had left around his face.

Yvonne blew out a large puff of air. At last, something concrete, but she was too upset to feel vindicated. Another death was not how she would have chosen to have her suspicions confirmed. However, now she might have enough to get the DCI to throw some resources her way. Perhaps this would enable her to bring on board her best friend. If Carwyn's suspicions were confirmed by Hanson, the investigation could begin in earnest.

"Any obvious injuries?"

Carwyn shook his head. "None that I could see. Perhaps, when his clothes are removed…"

"Thank you." Yvonne grabbed Carwyn by the shoulder.

"You're welcome." Carwyn nodded. "You been waiting for this?"

"I've had my suspicions. So many bodies-"

"I agree. We've never seen the like. Perhaps very rarely we've pulled out two or three bodies in the summer but, all the same demographic? Never. This is unprecedented."

"How old was this one?"

"Around twenty? Twenty two? Something like that. Very similar age to the others we've brought out. Like I say, same demographic. Something's definitely amiss."

Dewi joined them, having just had an earnest phone call. "I've got Jones and Clayton checking out possible identities. Hope to have suggestions in the next half hour."

Yvonne nodded. "That's great, Dewi. Let's get a picture of where and when this lad disappeared."

12

WILLIAM

"His name's William Henkel." DC Clayton wrote the name on the whiteboard, the rest of the team making notes. "He was here on a white-water rafting holiday, with friends. He's from the Birmingham area. His family have been located and informed."

"How long had he been missing?" Dewi scratched his head.

"About three weeks." Clayton folded his arms and leaned back on a desk. "His friends didn't report him missing straight away. It wasn't unusual, apparently, for him to meet a lady and go home with her. He'd had occasions, where he'd disappeared for a few nights, partying. His friends didn't become really concerned until the second week."

"I find it strange that his friends didn't worry about him for a whole week." Yvonne pursed her lip. "I get what you're saying about him having spent a night or two with a female before, but a week is a long time. Especially, when you're supposed to be white-water rafting with friends."

"I think they had begun to worry, ma'am, but were reluctant to report it to us. I get the impression that at least one of them had gone partying himself, and used hard drugs."

Yvonne sighed. "I'm going to the autopsy later today. If there's any sign of foul-play, I hope we find it. The divers seemed to think there's a chance he was dead before he went into the river. We need to go back to the night when his friends say they last saw him."

"Ma'am."

"What condition was he in? Was he drunk? Any drug use? I know toxicology will tell us what was found in the body, but water in the tissues will likely have watered it down."

"Well," Callum Jones took over the telling, walking up to the front. "That's where it all gets a little odd. According to one of his friends, he wasn't all that drunk. The other states that he was almost falling over."

"That's a helluva discrepancy. Why the difference?" Dewi folded his arms.

"Not sure, but independent witnesses described William as being fine when he left the Sportsman but, by the time he arrived at the Castle Vaults, some five minutes later, bouncers were, and I quote, 'unsure whether to let him in'."

"So, they thought he'd had a few too many."

"Right."

"Spiked?"

"Had to have been."

"Okay." It was Yvonne's turn to move to the front. "Dewi, we're going to the post-mortem this afternoon. If we get what I think we will, I'll go to the DCI with a view to getting a full task force set up. I believe we have a serial killer on our hands. I hope I'm wrong."

HANSON HAD COMMENCED THE POSTMORTEM, as Yvonne and Dewi, suitably covered, entered the mortuary. The sanitised smell of this clinical room would soon be replaced by the odour of death. The DI steeled herself for it.

"Of note," Hanson spoke loudly for the detectives and the tape, "is the lack of any obvious injury to the muscles of the chest, shoulders or neck, bruising might have been expected, if the subject had been fighting for a prolonged time, to stay afloat."

Yvonne's eyes strayed to those of the dead man. "Roger, can I ask you what you make of his eyes? Are they what you would expect for a drowning in a body of water?"

"Not exactly." Hanson shook his head. "I would have expected them to be more rounded and shiny. That being said, the body has been out of the water now for some twenty-four hours and this may have impacted on the eyes."

Hanson continued to talk for the tape, as he took samples, and excised organs for weighing.

Yvonne pulled her mask a little tighter, as the odour hit her hard.

"The stomach has some water present, but not as much as I would have expected, and there's no evidence of vomiting. I'm seeing only a relatively small amount of water in the lungs."

Yvonne frowned. "So, he couldn't have drowned in the river?"

"Well, I'm not saying that, at this point. But, it's suggestive of that possibility. A person can dry-drown, however. A spasm can block the lungs, resulting in choking for air, just like drowning. Being submerged in water can result in glottal spasm. But I was expecting more water in the stomach."

"I see."

"The other thing I'd say, is that there's an absence of anything in the hands of the victim. During accidental drowning, the victim will grab for anything they can to try and get a hold and pull themselves out. Sometimes, that's floating debris - twigs, grass...leaves. There's an absence of that, here."

Yvonne made notes.

"What I can say, is that blood pooling was not in the way I would have expected, if the victim had died in the water. Blood had congregated more in the back and buttocks region. The body of a person drowning in a river or pool of water, would generally be in a foetal position. The blood would pool in the areas underneath the corpse, pretty much keeping the body in that position. That did not happen in this case."

"On balance, Roger, would you say this man was dead before he went into the water?"

"I'd say so, Yvonne. But, I believe he did drown. I think he dry drowned somewhere else, in a bath, for example, and was then placed in the river. I'll have toxicology results tomorrow. I'll be able to tell you, then, how intoxicated he was."

"That's great." Yvonne was grateful of the chance to step back away from the table. But, she felt for the young man laid out there. Felt for his family. "I forgot to ask you." She paused and turned back to the pathologist. "Any sign of sexual activity?"

Roger shook his head. "None that I could detect."

13

THE PUSHER

DCI Llewellyn strode into the office and cleared his throat to get their attention. Unusually for him, he was in uniform.

"Everything all right?" Yvonne looked at him, wide-eyed.

"Has anyone here been talking to the press, ahead of the scheduled press conference?"

Yvonne shook her head with a frown. "No, of course not. At least, not that I am aware of."

"Then, what's this?" He tossed copies of the County Times and Shropshire Star onto her desk.

Yvonne quickly scanned the headlines. "Oh, no."

"Yeah. This is probably something we could do without."

Both papers had run with the same main story. Front page news. 'Has The Pusher come to Mid-Wales?'

Yvonne put both hands to her face. "Perhaps the family or friends have been talking to others. I mean, we're not going to be able to hide it, if we've got a killer on our hands."

"Yvonne." The DCI put his hands in his trouser pockets. "We have one unexplained death, which we can speculate *may* be a murder. We have verdicts of accidental deaths on three others. That does not mean we have a serial killer in our midst."

"I wanted to talk to you about that, sir. I think we very well may have a serial killer here in Mid-Wales. But I haven't spoken to the press, and I certainly am not suggesting it is an urban legend serial killer from the Manchester canals."

"Yvonne." He sighed. "I respect your opinion. You're one of my best officers but, really, this is a rural community. We don't have a serial killer hiding behind every corner. Although, I have to admit, you're pretty good at catching them when we do."

"Then trust me on this, sir. Let me set up a task force to look into these deaths, properly. Fully resourced. Let me make extended enquiries of family and friends, and let me set up structured surveillance."

"And what if you're wrong? It's going to cost, and it'll be my skin on the line."

"Some of these boys had arguments the night they disappeared. I've only just begun to look into that. If you like, I'll come with you to see the superintendent. I just won't be able to forgive myself if even one more young man dies in our rivers, this year. And I know," Yvonne nodded towards the papers, "they won't either."

LLewellyn ran a hand through his hair, his face drawn. "All right. Get a file with everything you know so far on my desk by the end of play today, and I'll speak with the super tomorrow morning. See what resources I can get for you. We'll have to put a time limit on it, though. There's no bottomless pit. At some point, you might want to liaise with Manchester. They've obviously been dealing with this type of speculation for some time. Might help us deal with it better."

"I'll do what I can, sir."

"Thanks."

"Oh, and sir?"

"Yes?"

"Thank you."

"Google is like having an extra copper on your team." Dewi grinned at her. "Look at this. Page after page dedicated to The Pusher. Where do you want to start?"

"Wikipedia," Yvonne asserted. "It's good for a general low-down on a subject."

"Righty-oh." Dewi typed into his laptop. "Oh, okay. Apparently it's a rock song written by Hoyt Axton. Oh no, it's not. It's a Swedish music group."

"Ha ha, very funny. And don't even mention drugs, or I'll wrap that bloody laptop round your neck."

Dewi laughed out loud. "Okay. Okay. The Pusher is a *proposed* serial killer responsible for a number of the eighty-plus deaths, around the Manchester canals, since 2004."

"Yes, well, we know that, Dewi. Get more specific."

"Right you are, ma'am. There's a psychologist-writer, a Thomas Sheridan, proposing that The Pusher is targeting homosexuals or men who look like they might be homosexual, as a means to control his own homosexual feelings."

They read through various articles, including some on other sites and it was clear that some of the victims had been subject to foul play or had open-verdicts on cause of death. It was also clear that some of the men were missing for days, weeks or even months, before their bodies were discovered. Rumours of abductions abounded.

"You don't really believe that a serial killer from Manchester is down here picking off our boys, do you?"

"No. I don't. I think we may have our very own version.

However, any hints and tips from that case *and* views of Manchester police would be useful, when looking at our own case."

"Except we're not sure we have a serial killer-"

"Neither are they, Dewi. And water deaths are some of the hardest to determine cause. But there are enough open verdicts and suspicious deaths to warrant serious attention. We know of actual serial killers who have disposed of bodies in water, in the belief that trace evidence will be washed away. It's not impossible that *we* have a killer looking to do the same. But, perhaps, ours enjoys drowning as some sort of psycho-sexual thrill. And, the homosexual angle, I hadn't considered that, but that's also a possibility."

"I guess we need to get on with interviewing witnesses and suspects?"

"Yes, we do, Dewi. Yes, we do."

14

ALTERCATIONS

"Come on then, Dewi. I think it's about time we made our way to Clive Jones' farm."

"Ma'am?" Dewi looked up in surprise.

"Well, we know foul-play was almost certainly involved in the death of William Henkel. We should go over all recent river deaths with a fine-toothed comb. Hannah told us that Clive Jones is the farmer who had an argument with her brother Lloyd, the night he disappeared. If nothing else, talking to Clive should give us a fuller picture of Lloyd's state of mind. *And* it could help us picture the events leading up to his disappearance and death."

"I'm with you." Dewi nodded. "That's if he'll talk to us."

"There's only one way to find out." Yvonne grabbed her bag and headed out.

Dewi shrugged at DC Clayton, grabbed his jacket, and ran out after her.

Yvonne took her wellingtons out of the boot. The ground wasn't that soft, but the track was littered with sheep droppings and cow pats and she didn't fancy it on her shoes, or in the footwell of her car. She looked down at Dewi's footwear.

He grinned and shrugged. "I'll take my chances. I can always wipe them on the grass if I step in anything."

She grinned. "Make sure you do, then."

A motorbike came tearing down the track, stopping with a skid a few feet away.

Yvonne held a hand to her chest, her breath caught in her throat.

"What the..." Dewi glowered at the rider, who was still wearing his helmet. "What d'you think you're doing?" he shouted, striding towards the intruder.

"Who are you? What are you doing on my land?" The voice was deep and cracked. The rider coughed.

Yvonne stepped forward. "We're police officers from CID, Newtown police station. I'm DI Giles and this is DS Hughes. Are you Clive Jones?"

He stared at her through the gap in his helmet, his eyes narrowed. "I might be. Why you asking?"

"We're investigating the death of Lloyd Jones. We believe you may have known him."

"What? Lloyd who fell in the river? Why you investigating that? He was drunk. We all seen it. He could barely keep himself upright by the time he left everyone. I'm not surprised he ended up in the river. Couldn't hold his drink."

Quite apart from the callous way he had referred to Lloyd's death, Yvonne felt a strong dislike developing in her gut, for reasons she couldn't quite put her finger on.

"You don't seem that concerned." She placed one hand on her hip, controlling her wayward hair with the other.

"Why would I be? I hardly knew him. Sure, when I heard, I felt a bit sorry for him. We all did. But, honestly?

Why go and hang around by the water when you've had that much to drink?"

"So, in your opinion, he was drunk enough to fall in?"

"I saw him wobbling around, yeah."

"You were witnessed having an argument with him. What was that all about?" Dewi took a couple of steps closer to the rider. "And could you take your helmet off for a minute?"

"Am I under arrest?"

"Is there a reason to arrest you?" Yvonne returned his stare, as he removed his helmet.

"No. You're asking a lot of questions." His hair had a significant amount of grey and appeared as though he hadn't had it cut in a while. His nose and cheeks had a ruddy hue. His skin was cracked and dry. His overalls were splashed with the muck expected from working on a farm.

"We're just trying to piece together his last movements. Trying to get an idea of his state of mind. So, tell us about the argument."

"It was nothing. Banter. You know. When us men have had a few drinks, we get a bit loud. There can be a bit of roughing about."

"Was there *roughing about* with Lloyd?"

"Not really."

"What did you say to him?"

"I asked him where his girlfriend was."

"That's it?"

"Yep. Pretty much."

"And what did he say?"

"I don't remember, exactly, but it was basically telling me it was none of my business."

Yvonne made a few notes in her pocketbook. "He was upset. He and Wendy had fallen out, earlier in the day."

"Yeah, well, she'd been cool with him for a while."

"Did he tell you that?"

"No. We could see it, when they were out together."

"Did you see them out together often?"

"Yeah."

"How well did you know Wendy?"

"She used to come and baby-sit, up at the farm."

"Your children?"

"Yes. They're in their late teens, now. Wendy used to look after them on a Friday night, if me and the missus went out together."

"How old was Wendy, when she baby-sat for you?"

He narrowed his eyes at her. "Sixteen when she started coming, and eighteen when she stopped."

"Did you stop needing her?"

"Lloyd didn't like her coming. She stopped when they got together."

"But your children don't need sitters now-"

"It wasn't her choice to stop coming. It was his."

"Did you resent him for that?"

"He had no idea how to treat her. He was jealous."

"Of what?"

Clive fell silent.

Yvonne frowned. "I'm curious as to why witnesses said you'd had an argument, if that was all that was said."

"Yeah, well, there was a bit of back and forth. He gave me a shove. I shoved him back. He wasn't very steady on his feet."

"Where did the argument occur?"

"I dunno. Castle...I think."

"What time did you leave the Castle?"

"I left when they threw us out."

"What time was that?"

"By time we left, probably about one o'clock. Maybe just after."

"Where did you go then?"

He leaned back on his bike. "I thought you were interested in *his* state of mind?" The muscles in his face had stiffened.

"Did you go home?"

"No. I went to the nightclub with my mates."

"Crystals?" Yvonne held her tongue. He seemed a little old for that nightclub's clientele.

"Yes."

"Stay there long?"

"About an hour."

"You like music, then."

"I sometimes feel like continuing the party, when I've had a few. Don't we all?"

"When was the last time you saw Lloyd?"

"Last time I saw him was in the Castle. He must have left before me. I didn't see him leave. By that time, I wasn't paying him any attention."

Yvonne cast her eyes around the green rolling hills and the woods, just beyond where they stood. The air was permeated by the rich sound and smell of animals. "I bet this is a lovely place to farm." Her eyes came back to Clive Jones.

"Been in my family for generations. It's in our blood. Can't imagine doing anything else." His body relaxed. "Do you like what you do?" he asked, spitting a couple of feet to his left.

Yvonne flinched. "It's a compulsion." She folded her arms. "If you remember anything else from that night, I'd like you to call us at the station. Ring 101 and ask for DI Giles or DS Hughes."

"Sure. Can I go, now?"

"You've always been free to go. Thanks for talking to us."

He kick-started his motorbike and turned it back up the field, kicking up the dirt as he went.

"Why do I have a niggling suspicion he likes young girls?" Yvonne pursed her lips.

"Perhaps we should ask Wendy what she really thinks of him?" Dewi offered, already picking his way back to the car.

Yvonne smiled, as she watched him gingerly trying to avoid the excrement. "Next time, bring your wellies."

15

ROB DAVIES

They drove up New Road, until it joined with Llanidloes Road, aiming for the roundabout at the top of town. A right turn brought them to the campus of Newtown College.

Rob Davies had agreed to meet them at the Cwm Harry allotments, where he had been helping out occasionally, between lectures.

He was waiting at the allotment gates. Although dressed casually, in jeans and a hoody, his clothing had the appearance of quality and he appeared smart, with an air of confidence which belied his nineteen years. His mid-length brown hair was tied in a small ponytail.

"Rob Davies?" Yvonne called out, as she fiddled with the gate latch.

"That's me." He came over to help her.

In the distance, the DI could see an array of polytunnels. "Thank you," she said.

"You wanted to talk to me about James?"

"Yes." Yvonne introduced herself and Dewi, but Rob knew their names from the note he'd been given.

He smiled and nodded, before placing the knuckle of his right forefinger in his mouth. "Caught it on thorn." He grimaced. "Keep getting stuff in it and it stings like hell."

He led them to a couple of seats near a shed, and motioned for them to sit. "I was really sorry to hear about James. We didn't always see eye-to-eye, but what happened to him..." His voice trailed away and he turned his gaze to the trees in the distance.

That was something, at least. His wistfulness appeared genuine. Yvonne sighed. "It's a terrible tragedy. And I don't mean that to sound glib. He was so young and that was no way to die."

"No." Rob shook his head. "How can I help? If there's anything I can do, I will."

"Thanks." Dewi sat with his legs stretched out in front of him. "We just wanted to ask you a few questions about the night James was last seen."

"Okay. Fire away."

Yvonne opened her pocket book and licked the end of her pen, to get the ink flowing. "How long had you known James?"

"Oooh, about eight years, give-or-take. We were in high school together."

"Were you friends in school?"

"We were. We weren't best friends or anything, but we hung out in the same groups, played football and hung around the playground together. Didn't usually see much of him outside of school unless we were involved in the same sports match. We were in the high school football team. James even had trials with a premier league club."

"He did?"

"Yeah. Liverpool. I'm not sure, but they may even have

offered him an apprenticeship there, but he didn't take it. That was the rumour, anyway."

"Why didn't he take it?"

"Sally."

"His girlfriend?"

"That's right. She's a couple of years older than him, and she'd already started college, here, at the campus behind you. He didn't want to leave her or disrupt her education, so he made the decision to go to college, himself."

"Thoughtful young man."

"Yeah. Yeah, he was." Rob stared at the ground, his eyes glazed.

"So, tell me about the night James was last seen alive." Yvonne's pen paused over the page, her eyes studying the young man in front of her.

"It was a typical Friday night, really. There were about ten of us, altogether, out in town. We drank in the Buck and the Exchange, the Elephant and Castle, the Sportsman, and finished up in the Castle Vaults."

"Did you notice anything unusual about James that night?"

"Not really, no. I mean we were all getting merry as we usually do."

"Did you have an argument with James that night?"

Rob sighed. "I did...I did." He ran his hands through his hair. "I really wish I hadn't. If only I could go back."

"What was it about?"

"Something stupid. Silly."

"Go on."

"Well, like I say, we were merry and well on our way to being drunk." He ran his hands through his hair again. "James wolf-whistled a couple of girls in the bar at the Sportsman. It probably wasn't anything more than a bit of banter, but, for some reason, I got annoyed at it. I'm not a fan of wolf-whistling girls, anyway, but I was aware that Sally doted on him, and I reminded him that she was at home waiting."

"How did he take it?"

"He got upset, and accused me of wanting her for myself. Said I hadn't got over her leaving me for him. Truth is, he was probably right."

"You used to be an item with James' girlfriend?"

"Back in high school, yes. She was my first love, actually. She was just starting sixth form when we got together. I was just beginning my GCSE courses. She was sixteen and I was fourteen. We never did any more than kiss, but we'd spend a lot of time talking about the things that interested us. She's a good debater."

"So, you were still with Sally when James began to see her?"

"She finished with me before she started dating him. She told me I was too young for her. James was a year older than me. And that was that."

"You took it hard?"

"Cried my eyes out. For a few months I hated him. But I got over it. I still missed her, but, she was right. At the time, I was too young."

"What happened, when he got upset?"

"We squared up to each other. Started pushing each other around. Our friends told us to cut it out and then the barman came from behind the bar to tells us to pack it in or leave."

"The barman...you mean Geoff Griffiths?"

"Yes, Geoff Griffiths." He rubbed his chin. "It's funny, I'd seen Geoff staring over at James a few times, while we were in there. Watching him intently. Like maybe he was expecting him to cause trouble, at some point."

"Do you think that was why he had been so quick to appear from behind the bar?"

"I do."

"Had James caused trouble in the Sportsman before?"

"I don't recall him ever having done so. I mean, James would get a bit loud occasionally, singing and stuff. Perhaps, that was it. He was getting a little bit too loud, like wolf-whistling the girls, etc."

"You said that Geoff told you to 'pack it in and leave'," Yvonne read from her notes. "Did he say anything, specifically, to James?"

"He grabbed his arm and told him he'd had enough. I was a bit surprised by that, because I didn't think James was that drunk. Not at *that* time."

"Did you see James after the argument?"

"Yes, we all went to the Castle, but I don't remember James being there for very long. He disappeared and I didn't see him go. None of us saw him go. He certainly didn't make an effort to say goodnight to any of us, that I recall."

"And, you didn't see him again after that?"

"No. The next time I saw him was when his picture was being shared all over Facebook, saying he'd disappeared and asking if anyone had seen him. I kept an eye out, but thought he'd probably ended up going home with someone. I didn't think too much of it. But his body was found floating in the river and I realised just how serious the situation had been." James shook his head. "Unbelievable, really."

"Would you say, in your opinion, that he had been drunk enough to fall in the river accidentally?"

"Well, that's the odd part. Although he was on his way to

getting drunk in the Sportsman, he wasn't stumbling around, he was holding himself fine. But, when I saw him briefly in the Castle, he looked pretty far-gone. Couldn't have been more than half-an-hour in between. He seemed to get very drunk very quickly, and then, yes, I could have envisaged him having an accident in that state. If he'd come to say goodbye, I'd have suggested he get a taxi, or that one of us saw him home."

"Really?"

"Really. I know we'd argued, but I would never have wished what happened to him on anyone. Whether-or-not they'd previously stolen my girlfriend."

Yvonne nodded. She gave a shiver, as she caught the first hint of Autumn. The air had cooled considerably. Above them, clouds covered any blue sky that had been left over from the morning. The DI wished she had brought a more substantial coat.

"Thank you, Rob. We may need to talk to you again." Her hip clicked, as she raised herself from the chair. She felt a twinge in her lower back, as she straightened up.

"Anytime, Inspector. Anytime."

16

SECRETS OF THE RIVER

The dank morning air spiked the hairs on her arms and neck. A curling mist stealthily rose from the river. Without closing her eyes, Yvonne could still see Lloyd and William's bodies floating on the surface of the water. Her own body shuddered, involuntarily.

Footsteps coming from behind had her swinging around to her right. A smiling Tasha, holding a fresh coffee in each hand, approached along the path. "Jumpy?" She held out one of the coffees, which the DI gratefully accepted.

"I was deep in thought. Autumn's here, already."

"I know. Just look at that mist. After what I've been hearing about this river, I'm not sure I'd want to be here alone."

Yvonne grimaced. "At this time, you'd probably be safe enough. But, at just gone midnight? After you'd had a few? Perhaps, a different story."

Tasha took a gulp of her coffee. "After this, I'll be fully awake." She replaced the lid. "So, what are we doing out here at seven am?"

"I'm going to ask for you to be officially in on this case. I'll ask Llewellyn this morning. "

"Okay, and?"

"And I just wanted to get my thoughts straight before I do. I have to make sure I get my points across, and that my thoughts are not a jumbled mess. I think someone is drowning young men in the river, or killing them first and then dumping the bodies in the river. I wanted to run everything past you, so I have a working theory to run past the DCI."

She proceeded to fill Tasha in on the postmortem results for William Henkel, finishing with, "He was killed on land and then placed in the water."

"Someone obviously covering their tracks." Tasha pursed her lips. "Do you know where he went in?"

"Not yet. I thought we could wander along and get into the head of his killer. Maybe that would help us with determining the possible dumping places. I suspect we'd be looking at somewhere close to a road or car park. Somewhere close to the water, without too much risk of discovery."

Tasha pressed her lips together and tilted her head to one side. "How'd he choose this victim?"

"William was last seen by friends in town, following a night out."

"Okay, so similar to the other recent deaths?"

"Right."

"Did the killer abduct him? Or, did he lure him home with the promise of more alcohol? Just a thought, but did the pathologist test for drugs?"

"We're awaiting a full toxicology report. I've requested they test for GHB, amongst other things, even though I know that it disappears from the system very quickly. There might still be a trace."

"It would be hard to abduct a fit young man, unless he was extremely intoxicated, drugged, or went willingly."

"Or there was more than one perp. You know, a date rape drug would explain the seemingly intoxicated state of at least two of the other victims. Both of them went from tipsy to legless in around thirty minutes."

"Do you know anything about William's sexuality?"

"Not yet, the team are talking to his friends and family. But, I do know that other recent drowning victims were straight. Or, at least, they definitely had steady girlfriends."

"Okay, but it wouldn't be unheard of for seemingly straight men to have gay sex or even be bisexual."

"Yes. Nothing's ruled out at this stage. What I will say, however, is we've found no evidence of any sexual interference with the victims. You know the locals have begun to compare this to the Manchester canal deaths. They are even speculating that The Pusher is staying around here."

"The pusher being the urban-legend killer that has been ruled out by police authorities?"

"Yes. Any more deaths and we might be facing local hysteria. I can just see the DCI loving that."

"There've been several deaths in Bristol, too. Again, no official acceptance of any serial killer theory but the locals are up in arms." Tasha took another couple of swigs of her coffee. Her coffee-heated breath formed white clouds as she spoke. "Not only that, but young men have been turning up in the northern United States, around Interstates 90 and 94. Places like Minnesota and Wisconsin. All college age men, many of them very bright and athletic. Many actual college students. There are some who believe there is a network of killers, they've dubbed the Smiley Face Killers. It's not an officially held view. At least, if it is, no-one in authority is admitting it. The claim is that like-minded killers are talking to each other over the internet, on the dark web. They egg each other on to go and kill."

Yvonne shook her head. "If we are losing so many young men that people are seriously questioning what is going on, then maybe we *are* looking at something more than just accidental deaths in some of these cases."

"Perhaps. I know that there have been many open verdicts on these deaths. Cause undetermined. Including many of the Manchester canal deaths."

Yvonne shivered, both hands gripping the still-warm cup of coffee. "Let's hope it's nothing so organised as a web of killers. That would be a terrifying prospect."

Tasha nodded. "But, for a lot of drowning cases, the answers will of course be mundane. Accident, suicide, an attempting to swim whilst too intoxicated."

"Yes, well, we have one homicide that we know of, and potentially at least two more. Wait a minute, you said Smiley Face Killers. Why are they called Smiley Face?"

"They allegedly leave graffiti of smiley-face emojis where the victims are thought to have entered the water."

"Oh." Yvonne frowned, looking at the ground.

"What is it?" Tasha tilted her head, trying to get a look at the DI's face.

"Probably nothing, but I saw the chalked Roman numeral for two on an ash tree close to where Lloyd Jones' phone was found. I was convinced that someone had set that up to mislead us as to where he went in. He just didn't have the injuries to support slipping and falling into the water via those boulders at the bottom. If we have one killer, Lloyd would have been the second victim."

Tasha looked wide-eyed at the DI. "Really?"

"Really."

"Well, the Roman numeral is unlikely to have been left by the killer, if it is not actually the place where Lloyd went in."

"Except, there is another scenario." Yvonne frowned. "What if Lloyd was led down the bank, in his intoxicated state, and his head held under the water until he was dead?"

"Woah. Wouldn't that have left tell-tale signs?"

"I don't know. I'll write it in my notepad and ask Hanson later."

"Where do you think William went in?"

"SOCO and Hanson are working on the likely distances his body travelled after rising to the surface. They're looking at river height and flow-rates etc, to come up with likely entry points. They'll have search teams out combing the banks when they have an idea. I just thought I might get a head start by looking at spots where the road isn't too far away from the river. Like I say, if William was already dead, the killer had to carry his body. He wouldn't have wanted to do that for any significant distance."

"Okay. I don't know this area that well."

"Looking at Google maps, I saw two possible places within five miles from where he was found. One was not far from here, located near Vaynor housing estate, in Newtown. The other was five miles away, in Caersws. I think Vaynor is a strong candidate because the river is deep enough for the body to sink. I'm told there are eddying currents there, too. Caersws, I'm not so sure. I might leave that one to river experts to check out."

"Wanna take a look up Vaynor area, now?" Tasha nodded in the direction of the main car park. "My car's over there."

"Let's go."

17

SWIRLS AND EDDIES

They parked the car just off the main road and headed towards Vaynor top field. From there, it was a relatively short distance to the river. The approach was shielded by thick bushes and tree cover. This could be the ideal place for the murderer to dispose of the body.

Yvonne looked across at Tasha, who was standing, hands on hips, lips pursed. "Good candidate?"

"I'd say so." Tasha headed for the tree line.

"One moment, Tasha." Yvonne placed a hand on her arm. "Let's not take the direct route. If this was the dump site chosen by the killer, he would have likely taken the shortest route possible to the river. Let's go the long way round. If we're right, SOCO will be hacked off if we've tramped all over any evidence."

Tasha nodded. "Of course."

They followed the hedge line as closely as they could, Yvonne keeping an eye out for anything that could be possible evidence. A squashed and dirty plastic bottle and faded crisp packet was all she'd seen so far. Both of which were unlikely to have been left there in the right time frame. Even so, she gave them a wide birth. As they approached the tree-line, she paused, looking for a likely entryway. A place where someone could carry a body through, whilst not being too hampered by brush and branches.

"I reckon those are the two most likely routes. What do you think?" The DI pointed them out to Tasha.

The psychologist nodded."They look good to me."

Yvonne stopped before going through the first one and looked back in the direction of the housing estate. "You know, this is not particularly overlooked at all." There was a two-foot wide dirt patch, where nothing much was growing. She suspected that children from the estate must come down here reasonably regularly. But at night, it would be almost pitch black. Good cover for a killer.

Once through the bushes, the ground banked straight down, only a few feet to the river. Yvonne put both hands deep in her trouser pockets, leaning on one leg. "This is as far as we should go, just in case." Her voice was soft. "But, I think this place is ideal. The river looks deep here. I'll request that SOCO take a look."

"Wait a minute." Tasha stared at a place just above the DI's head and pointed. "Look."

Yvonne swung round, eyes rapidly searching for what Tasha was looking at. Her heart thumped in her chest, her breathing more rapid. "Oh my god." She was open-mouthed.

"The Roman numeral for four." Tasha's eyes were alive. "Didn't you say that William was victim number four?"

"I did. He was. Steven Bryant was victim number three."

"Looks like thick chalk."

"I think this is the place." Yvonne took out her mobile and took photographs.

"I'm guessing we can't go down to the waterline?" Tasha grimaced. She already knew the answer.

The DI shook her head. "No. Not yet. But we'll get these photographs back to the station and compare with those I took of the chalked two lines, where Lloyd's phone was found. If this is what I think it is, then there'll be a one-stroke chalk mark where James was found.

18

A GARBLED MESSAGE

There was sweat on Dewi's forehead and upper lip and his tie was unusually loose, as Yvonne and Tasha headed into CID.

"You okay, Dewi?" Yvonne searched his face.

"Where have you been? I've been looking for you all over."

"Oh." The DI looked taken aback. "Well, why didn't you call me?"

"I did. Three times." Dewi took a couple of deep breaths.

The DI pulled her mobile out of her bag. Sure enough, there were three missed calls."Oh, so you did. Sorry. Must have been in a bad signal area." She shrugged. "Come on, then. What's up?" She ran an impatient hand through her hair.

"One of James Owen's friends has been in touch. We've got his mobile phone. He thinks James left him a message the night he disappeared?"

"What?" Yvonne looked at him, wide-eyed. "Well, where is it? Why are we only hearing about this, now?"

"The friend's phone has been playing up, or so he says,

and he wasn't able to access his voicemail. When he finally did, he had half a dozen massages, including one he thinks came from James."

"What do you mean, he thinks? Didn't he check the number?"

"Yeah. But, like I said, he had a load of messages and the phone's playing up."

"Okay."

"We've sent it for a forensic clean-up and production of a digital copy. However, good ole Clayton has made a copy for us to be going on with. It's on his laptop. We've just been listening to it. Wanna hear?"

"Is the pope catholic? Of course I want to hear. Let's go."

Clayton, Dewi, Yvonne and Tasha crammed around the laptop on Clayton's desk. Clayton had been listening through earphones. He took them out. "I thought we could all listen together, then take turns at listening through these. He held up the phones. Maybe write down what we think we hear. That way, we can compare. I'll warn you, ma'am, it's not easy to decipher."

Yvonne nodded. "Okay, go for it."

Yvonne leaned her head forward and down, straining to make out the words. The caller sounded under the influence and was speaking fast, almost running his words into each other. He sounded out of breath. Her overall impression was that he was scared of something or someone.

"Can you play it again?" she asked, as the call came to an abrupt end.

"Sure." Clayton pressed the replay symbol.

'*Illegible, illegible*, are you there? Where are you? I'm *illegible, illegible* the bridge. There's someone *illegible, illegible* me. I can't *illegible, illegible, illegible* the roundabout. Are you in town? I *illegible* police.' The caller had paused speaking at this point, and a loud and fast breathing could be heard, followed by a muffled sound - almost as though the caller had hurriedly placed the phone in his pocket. More words followed, possibly a short conversation, but these were so muffled they were impossible to decipher.

Dewi sighed, "I think he may have put his phone on loud speaker at the end, 'cos I swear I can hear two voices."

Yvonne nodded. "Me too, but I think he may have put his phone in his pocket, or held it too tightly. I can't hear what they're saying."

"Want to try the headphones now?" Clayton plugged them into the laptop and passed them to her.

"Thank you." Yvonne placed them over her ears, and closed her eyes.

'Pete, *illegible*, are you there? Where are you? I'm crossing *illegible, chased?...over* the river. There *someone? something? Illegible, illegible,* me. I can't get *illegible, illegible,* the round-about. Are you in town? I *heard? need?* Police.'

The DI requested she listen to it one more time and wrote down what she thought he was saying. Afterwards, the others took their turns, each writing down what *they* thought had been said.

"Okay, let's compare notes." Yvonne threw her pad onto the table. "That's my take on it. Anyone got anything different or anything to add?"

"I got, 'please', not Pete." Dewi frowned. "The friend's name is Mark."

"I heard, 'please', too." Tasha nodded.

"Oh." Clayton frowned. I heard, 'yes.'

This was the pattern throughout the listened-to voice-mail. There were a number of differences between their versions. However, they agreed that James sounded drunk, scared, and out of breath.

"Okay. Okay. We had better wait until we get the cleaned-up version. I hope they can get it clearer than that, or we've got no hope of knowing what he actually said. Why didn't his phone company let us know that he made a phone call that night?" Yvonne pursed her lips.

"Truth is, ma'am, no-one asked them. His death was, still is, deemed an accidental death-by-drowning and the phone records were not checked."

"And James' phone is still missing..."

"Yes, as is his jacket and wallet." Dewi folded his arms. It's not a lot to go on, but it's something."

"It is, Dewi. Good work. Can we talk to the friend? Informal interview? I feel uncomfortable with the 'my voice-mail hasn't been working properly for two months' explanation. It may be true, but I'd still like to speak with him about it face-to-face."

"I'll arrange it, ma'am. His name is Mark Evans. He seemed pretty upset. I think he holds himself partly responsible for what happened to James." Dewi sighed.

Yvonne raised her eyebrows.

"Because he didn't receive the call and because he was the last person to see James alive."

"I see. Well, he's a person of interest at the very least. Let's get him in."

"Will do."

"Oh, and Dewi?"

"Ma'am?"

"CCTV footage was taken from some of the cameras in town from the night James disappeared. Did anyone actually take a look at it?"

"Not sure. I don't think so. It was asked for, because he was missing. But, he was found in the river, so-"

"I know. I know. Death by accidental drowning." Yvonne

sighed. "Clayton, can you see if you can get hold of the footage? I think we need to have a good look. Something was clearly happening, possibly by the bridge. We should go through every piece of footage that was seized."

"I'll hunt it down, ma'am. It's most likely bagged up in the evidence room."

"Thanks, Clayton."

19

SIDETRACKED

"Come in."

Yvonne swallowed hard. The DCI sounded impatient. Something he rarely ever did. She smoothed down her skirt and opened the door to his office, poking her head through with a grimace.

"Ah, Yvonne. Come on in, will you?"

"Is everything okay, sir?" she asked, taking the seat the other side of his desk.

"I was about to ask you the same question." His eyes locked onto hers.

She shifted in her seat. "We're getting on with things, sir." She took in his neat hair and very straight tie.

"Any news on the hit-and-run?"

Yvonne felt her heart sink. She so wanted to solve that case but they had so little to go on as it was sheer slog for the officers who were going through relevant vehicles and checking their recent histories. "It's taking time, sir. But with every passing day, we're getting-"

"Nowhere?" He finished for her.

She glared at him. "That's unfair. There are uniformed

and CID officers working their butts off out there, desperately trying to find the vehicle. You know how little we had to go on."

"Problem is-" He folded his arms. "One of my best investigators has gotten a little side-tracked."

She rubbed her chin.

"I know you now have a possible murder to investigate, in William Henkel, but I have grieving parents wanting to know what we have. And it's not much."

Yvonne tilted her head to one side. "I'll go talk to them again. Explain."

"Please do." His face softened, somewhat. "Then, there's this." He pulled out a copy of the County Times from his desktop drawer.

Yvonne stared at the massive headline. 'Has The Pusher claimed four victims in Mid-Wales?' A photograph of James Owen smiled out at her from the page. A sub-heading of 'Was James the first victim?' had her breathing rapidly.

"I'm sorry, sir. I have no idea how this got out. Unless..."

"Unless what?"

"Unless James' friend, Mark Evans, spoke to the papers about his voicemail message."

"What voicemail message?" Llewellyn placed both hands behind his head.

"I was going to fill you in about that this afternoon, sir." Yvonne leaned forward in her chair, as she related the contents of the tape and the reasons for its late discovery.

He appeared genuinely interested, getting up and walking over to his window. "And you say he sounded afraid?"

"Very much so. He also sounded as though he'd been chased, and towards the end of the message I think he was talking to someone. We're getting the message cleaned up, so we can listen again."

He turned to face her, hands now in his pockets. "Those sharp instincts of yours are a precious addition to this team." He folded his arms. "I'm willing to go along with this."

"We've already set up an incident room, for William's death. Are you saying we can expand this to all the river deaths?"

"I think, given what we now know, we have to. *But*, ask your team to keep a lid on those deaths where we haven't had any evidence of foul-play. I don't want the families upset unnecessarily, and I do not want mass hysteria to hit the town as a whole."

Yvonne looked down at the paper.

The DCI followed her eyes. "*That*, not withstanding."

"There's something else." Yvonne bit her lip.

"Go on."

"If I deem it necessary, could I bring Tasha Phillips on board."

"Your psychologist friend?"

"Yes."

"I'll speak to the super about the budget and let you know."

Yvonne smiled. "Thank you, sir."

20

THE HOODED MAN

Dai Clayton signed for the evidence bag containing four CCTV compact discs, and climbed the stairs to CID. He set the bag down on his desk and cut the plastic clip.

There were no cameras down by the river. However, the three discs contained the footage from three of the town cameras and footage from inside the Castle Vaults public house. The town cameras covered the areas near long Bridge and the street which separated the Sportsman from the Castle. He took his jacket off and rolled up his sleeves. Callum had offered to help and was making them both a strong coffee. There would be hours of footage to sift through. This would be a Long haul.

"What took you so long?" he asked, pulling a chair up for Callum, as the latter returned with the strong coffees.

"Quick fag." Callum grimaced. "Sorry, mate."

Dai laughed. I forgot you're back on 'em. You have the will power of a gnat."

Callum shrugged. "Do gnats have will power?"

"No."

"Oh."

Dai flicked the mouse to get rid of the screensaver and loaded the first CD into his laptop. "Here we go."

"Shall I go get some crisps?" Callum asked.

Dai was about to say no, but thought better of it. "Sure, I'm a bit peckish too. I'll make a start. Make mine smoky bacon."

"Will do."

Dai checked the description for what James had been wearing the night he disappeared. Jeans, white Nike trainers and a black leather jacket over a black-and-white striped rugby-style shirt. He was five-foot-nine and weighed around two hundred pounds.

They were interested the time between ten and eleven pm, when James would have been leaving the Sportsman to go to the Castle, and the hour before and after midnight. They didn't have exact times for any of James' movements, as they were purely going on witness estimates and those witnesses were, themselves, under the influence at the time, so could not be exact.

By the time Callum returned, Dai had almost finished his coffee and was busily forwarding through the first camera footage.

"Got him yet?" Callum tossed two packets of crisps onto Dai's desk.

"Not yet. Just had a bunch of lads leaving the Sportsman, but he wasn't among them." Dai passed the description of James to Callum for him to get up to speed.

Callum opened his crisps and began munching, leaning forward to peer at the screen.

Dai shot shot him a look. "Do you have to crunch those in my ear?"

"Sorry." Callum grinned and pulled back.

"There. There." Dai pointed his pen at the screen, double checking the description to make sure he had it right. "That's him. That's James. There he is, leaving the Sportsman on his own at...ten fifty-eight pm. You can plainly see the black-and-white shirt to the front and, it's clear, he was still wearing his jacket at that stage."

"Seems a bit confused." Callum leaned forward again. "Look, he's stopped."

They watched the man on the screen taking his phone out of his pocket and checking it. He appeared unsteady and was turning in circles, looking all about him.

"What's he doing?" Dai frowned at the screen.

"I dunno, but he doesn't look that great. Maybe, he was more drunk than people gave him credit for."

The man on screen put his phone away, and began walking in the direction of the Castle Vaults. He stumbled up the steps, and one of the bouncers appeared to briefly check him over.

"We need to speak to that bouncer." Callum crunched another crisp and washed it down with coffee. "See if we can jog his memory and get him to give us his take on James' condition."

"If he'll talk to us. Folks can get jumpy about losing their licences."

"Still..."

"Yes. I agree. We need to talk to him."

"Wait a minute, who's that?" Callum pointed at the screen. "Rewind it a couple minutes, can you?"

"Okay, say when."

"There. There."

Callum pointed to a hooded figure, possibly slight taller than James, although it was hard to tell. He was heading along the same street and appeared to pause, when James paused. It was hard to make out exactly what the following man was wearing, but it appeared to be dark trousers and dark, hooded jacket.

"Why's he got his hood up in summer?" Callum leaned back in his chair.

"This was early summer. If I remember rightly, it was cool for the time of year. It's possible that the person's cold. But, I agree, it's possible he's following James. That pause was a bit odd."

"Oh, no." Callum sighed. "He's walked straight past. I was sure he was going to follow James in."

Dai rubbed his chin. "Me too."

"Oh, hang on. He's taken a right turn. That'd be the alleyway down the side of the Castle."

"So, he could be entering via the back door."

"Where all the smokers congregate."

"Right."

"Well, let's take a gander at the inside footage. You got that?"

"Yeah." Dai swapped the CDs over and forwarded the footage to the relevant timeframe.

The two of them proceeded to scour the crowd inside the pub for the hooded man.

"I don't see him. Do you?" Callum had stopped crunching crisps, desperately trying to spot the man they had seen outside.

Dai shook his head. "I'll bet he took his coat off. Anyone with malicious intent would be very aware of where the cameras are. There's James, talking to some people at the bar. He's just ordered a pint."

They watched James take his pint over towards the

dance floor, where he began chatting to a girl he appeared to know. Their glimpses of him were intermittent due to the number of people around, and it was mostly his upper body they caught sight of.

"He's definitely appearing unsteady on his feet there." Dai rewound the footage a little.

"I'm pretty sure that girl just stopped him from falling."

"We have a statement, in the file, from a girl who was in the Castle. I think that was probably her.

"Fast forward to when he leaves." Callum finished his coffee in a couple of mouthfuls.

Dai forwarded the footage to when James was downing the dregs of his beer. Someone bumped into him and James staggered back, before waving to the guy who appeared to apologise.

"Was that our guy?" Callum asked.

"I don't think so." Dai shook his head. "He looks a little small to be the man we saw earlier." James made his way towards the back of the pub and disappeared into the crowd at the back, where the toilets and back door were situated.

"I think that must be where he leaves." Dai ejected the CD and reached for the third disk. "We should be able to pick him up on this, once he's back on Broad Street and heading to the bridge."

When they picked him up again, James was back on Broad Street and looking increasingly unsteady on his feet.

"You see?" Callum scratched his head. "I'd say he's definitely drunk enough to fall in the river. Maybe the DI's barking up the wrong tree. This one really could have been an accident."

"You ever been that drunk before?" Dai turned to Callum, one eyebrow raised.

"Well, yeah a few times. Mostly when I was younger."

"You ever fall in a the river?"

"Er...no."

"Look, I'm not saying it doesn't happen, but falling into the river isn't *that* likely an outcome. Well, not in my opinion, anyway."

"There he is going over the bridge and looking down at the water."

They watched, as James continued unsteadily over the bridge and towards the roundabout at the top, at which point, he seemed to turn right. The next camera, near the hospital road, never picked him up. It had been studied at length, at the time of his disappearance. It had been thought that he may have changed his mind and doubled back, taking the opposite road off the roundabout and heading up Milford Road. There, he may have become lost and ended up taking a left, down through a cul-de-sac and into Dolerw public park, through which the River Severn ran. There were no cameras on Milford Road. What they could say, without a shadow of a doubt, is that a hooded man, very possibly the same hooded man from earlier, had followed James over the bridge. He had caught up with and overtaken the lad and headed right. He, too, was not picked up again by the camera near the hospital. The final disc had no secrets to give up.

"If we put this together with the voicemail, I think we can come up with a better understanding of what might have happened to James. We should take this to Yvonne." Dai leaned back in his chair. "I think James may have been abducted."

Yvonne thanked Callum and Dai for the hard work they had put in the CCTV footage. She studied it herself, with Dewi, and had to agree that the hooded man had to be someone of interest. Although they couldn't rule out accidental death, something in her gut told her there was more to it. This was reinforced the following day, when the toxicology results for Steven Bryant came through.

The DI ran to her bag, which lay on her desk, and pulled out her bleating phone. It was Hanson. "Roger?"

"We got the toxicology results back from lab and I can tell you that traces of GHB were found in Steven Bryant's samples."

"GHB? Really?"

"Yes."

"So, he was spiked?"

"Quite likely."

"Wait, you're sure it was higher than naturally occurring levels?"

"Yes. It was about ten times any naturally occurring levels. I think we can deduce that Steven had willingly or unwillingly taken the drug, and that he went into the river not long afterwards."

"Could he have fallen in accidentally, after having the drug?"

"It's possible, but with the amount he had, I'd question whether he'd have been capable of walking very far, unaided. But, yes, whether he fell or was pushed, he wouldn't have been able to get himself out again. The levels of GHB were just too high."

"If I've got a serial killer on my hands," Yvonne turned to face the window, "I think he may have just made his first major mistake."

"I'd talk to his friend." Hanson grunted. "Find out if James was into GHB, and find out who supplies it."

"Thanks." Yvonne laughed.

"Sorry." Hanson laughed back. "I'm not trying to-"

"It's okay, Roger. I know. I appreciate your help. Keep the results coming."

CHRIS AND JENNY

Chris Halliwell and Jenny Hadley had barely two weeks left on their secondment with CID. They had been tasked with helping to trace the hit-and-run vehicle which killed Callum Jenkins.

Chris thought it would be a good idea to knock on doors around the estate again. "Something may have been missed. I say we go and talk to people at the same time of day that Callum was knocked down. Gives us a greater chance of talking to people who were around to witness something."

Jenny bit her lip. "I'm not sure. Officers went all over that estate in the two weeks after he was killed. Are you honestly telling me they missed something? And that was when it was really fresh in the people's minds."

Chris nodded. "I get what you're saying, Jenny, but how many times have you been asked something, given an answer, and then later wished you'd added something else? Maybe something you weren't sure of at the time?"

Jenny, nodded, nervously playing with her ponytail. "Well, yes. I-"

"Exactly. Everyone does it. In this case, it will have

played on their minds and they will probably be dying to tell it to someone. That someone is us."

"It's a big estate."

"Then we'd better get going."

"Shouldn't you check with the DI?"

"Er. Yes. We'd better. Come on."

YVONNE WAS FLICKING through file notes on the river deaths when Chris and Jenny burst in.

"Sorry to disturb you, ma'am." Chris gave her a wide smile and she was struck by how handsome he was. His face was honest and open. She mused that he'd make some young woman a fine husband one day, and wondered at the reasons he and the mother of his child were not together.

"That's okay. How can I help?" She put down the notes. "What's the excitement?"

Chris stepped to one side, allowing his colleague to relay their idea. Jenny smiled at him.

"Ma'am, we were thinking of questioning Garthowen residents again, this afternoon. About four o'clock. See if anyone has anything else to tell us. Maybe, something they missed at the time."

Yvonne leaned back in her chair, nodding. "Good idea. Can I make a suggestion?"

The two recruits nodded.

"That car was doing a helluva lick down that road. Perhaps, find out if they are aware of any anti-social drivers or anything that's happened before or since. I've got a feeling that won't have been the first time that driver went down that road, and perhaps has been down there since. He or she may be getting cocky again. Putting their foot down."

"Will do, ma'am." Chris looked like he'd won the lottery

and Yvonne laughed out loud. "Go on then, you two. Go and get something for us."

"WE'VE PULLED in Kenny Walters, like you asked, ma'am." Callum poked his head around the door.

"Where is he, Callum?" Yvonne looked up from her notes, putting down her pen.

"Interview room one."

"Great. Have Dewi meet me there in fifteen, will you? It won't do Kenny any harm to be kept waiting. Better make him cup of tea, though."

"Will do."

"Oh, and Callum?"

"Ma'am?"

"If he asks why he's here, tell him you don't know."

"Okay."

THE DI'S eyes were drawn to Kenny's crossed ankles, under the table. Although it appeared he had the latest trend in white training shoes, they were muddy - the laces ragged and nearly undone.

She looked up and found him glaring at her, arms folded in angry challenge. Strands of loose hair hung in front of his eyes like the bars of a cage. He occasionally brushed them away, only for them to fall back again. His shirt, like his shoes, spoke of living beyond his means. It was also at odds with his unkempt appearance and lack of personal hygiene.

"Thanks for coming in, Kenny." Yvonne and Dewi pulled out chairs and seated themselves.

"Didn't have much of a choice, did I?" His mouth had a pronounced pout and his arms remained folded, but he uncrossed his ankles and sat a little straighter.

"It's just a friendly chat, Kenny. No need to get upset." Dewi smiled, but his eyes remained serious.

"You're gunna accuse me of something, I know it. You lot got nothing better to do."

Yvonne gave an affected laugh and held her hands up. "You're absolutely right, Kenny. We looked at each other this morning and said, 'You know, there's so little crime to solve around here, we might as well pull in Kenny Walters and waste a couple of hours of our time winding him up.'" She shook her head. "What are we like?"

"Very funny."

"Oh yes, that's right. There's a shed-load of cases to solve and we are very busy people. We'll try not to keep you too long, Kenny, but if you've got information, we want it."

"I want a lawyer."

"What, even before you know what we want to talk to you about?"

"Yeah. You're gunna fit me up. I'm not talking without a lawyer present."

"Well, it's your lucky day. We've got a duty solicitor coming in to make sure we don't use thumb screws." Dewi's voice sounded unusually deep.

"Speaking of which." The out of breath voice came from the back, and a middle-aged, smart-suited man put his briefcase on the floor next to the desk, taking the available seat next to his client.

"Mr. Davies." Yvonne nodded. "Thanks for coming."

"Kenny." Davies nodded at his client, who barely looked at him but continued sulking.

"Kenny, this is an informal chat, really. We've been

speaking to our colleagues in the drug squad and your name came up in connection with GHB." Yvonne purposely studied her notebook. "Specifically, some was found, six months ago, along with a stash of mamba, under a car in an area in which you had just been chased."

Kenny flicked her a look. "That wasn't mine." He scowled, flicking his hand in a dismissive gesture at her notebook.

"You mean you got away with it because no-one witnessed you discarding it."

"Careful..." Davies warned.

"Kenny, we're not trying to get you. We'll leave that to the drugs squad." Yvonne leaned towards him. "We think young men are being given GHB before being purposely drowned in the river."

Kenny's eyes widened.

Yvonne sensed that he knew something. "Do you know of anyone acquiring GHB recently? Say in... ooh... the last six months?"

Kenny's eyes dipped to the table, they flicked a couple of times from side-to-side, before coming back up to the DI's.

"No."

"You sure about that?"

"Yeah." He said the words but appeared distracted, his eyes glazing over as though seeing another time and place. As though seeing someone else. "What young men?" he asked, suddenly.

"James Owen, for example."

"James?"

"You knew him?"

"No. Not really. But I heard about him going missing and then being found in the river." He shifted in his seat, running his hand through his hair a couple of times.

"Did you supply him with GHB?"

"Me? No. I didn't even know him. I just knew that his family had been looking for him and it was all in the papers, when he was found. He didn't use drugs, did he?" From Kenny's creased-up face, it appeared he didn't think so.

Yvonne shrugged. "We don't think so. We think he was given it in a drink and he was unaware."

Kenny stared at her, unspeaking.

She continued. "We think some of the other river victims may also have been given GHB." This wasn't exactly true, although tests for trace evidence were ongoing. Kenny didn't need to know that.

Kenny shook his head. He eyes were wide, his pupils dilated.

"We're looking to trace the batch of GHB it came from."

"Look, I don't know anything." He got out of his seat, his hands shaking.

"You okay, Kenny?" Dewi also stood, reaching an arm out towards Kenny.

Kenny slumped back in his seat. "I don't know anything."

Yvonne leaned back in her chair. "Okay, Kenny. I tell you what. Go have a think about it. If anything comes back to you, or you hear anything, give us a call."

AFTER KENNY and his solicitor had left, Yvonne shook her head at Dewi. "He knows something."

"I agree. I think he looked scared."

"Ask uniform to keep a discreet eye on him. Keep us up to date of where they see him. Oh, and suggest they do stop-and-search on sight."

"Right you are, ma'am."

Her eyes were wistful, as she put her hands up to cradle the back of her head, elbows jutting forward, as though to ward off the bad stuff. "How many young lives has he messed up, Dewi. Destroyed, physically and mentally. I don't know how he lives with himself."

Dewi shrugged. "He probably doesn't think about it. It's easy money for him."

CHRIS AND JENNY had spoken to around a dozen households in Garthowen and, as yet, had gained no new information.

"I don't think we're going to get anything from this." Jenny sighed, pausing before the gate of number fifty-five.

"Hey, come on." Chris put a hand on her shoulder. "We'll finish the last few houses in this row. If anyone saw anything, they'll likely be in this row. Any one of these houses could hold the key."

Jenny narrowed her eyes at him, but his enthusiastic approach was infectious. "Come on, then. Let's knock on the door."

The lady who greeted them was wearing an apron. The sides of her face and her hands were covered in flour, which she wiped away with a tea towel.

"Hello. I'm Chris Halliwell and this is Jenny Hadley. We're police officers on secondment to CID."

"What's up? Has something happened? It's not Steve, is it?" Her wide eyes had them quickly reassuring her.

"No. We've not come about anyone in your family." Chris tilted his head, his smile designed to settle her nerves. "We've come about the hit-and-run incident that resulted in Callum Jenkins' death."

"Oh. Oh, I see. Wel,l you'd better come in." She turned to lead them inside.

Chris flicked a quick look at Jenny. Being called in could be a good sign.

"We know that officers have already been speaking to residents in the area." Chris sat in the offered armchair, whilst Jenny took the couch. "But, we've been wondering if anyone had remembered anything else. Or perhaps, you may have seen something since that made you anxious about that road."

"Such as someone driving erratically or above the speed limit, Mrs Moore." Jenny readied her notepad.

The lady nodded. "Call me Sheena."

Chris noted her name into his pocketbook.

"There was something, but I don't know if it's relevant or not." Mrs Moore rubbed her cheek.

"Go on," Jenny encouraged.

"Well, I've seen a car racing down that road a fair few times. Mostly when it's getting dark or after it's dark."

"What sort of car, Sheena?"

"A light-coloured vehicle. Maybe silver. I'm not great with car models, I don't drive. But, a Nissan, maybe? Small, definitely. Maybe a Nissan Micra? Like I say, I'm not good with car models."

"Has anyone else in your family seen this car?" Chris searched Sheena Moore's face, his heart beating faster. "Someone who could recognise the model?"

"No. I don't think so." She shook her head.

"Could you ask your husband?"

"I could ask my husband and son, and let you know if either of them have seen it and recognise the model."

"We'd be so grateful, Mrs Moore. Did you by any chance take down a registration number?"

Sheena Moore shook her head. "I didn't, but I can tell you the year."

"Great, that's something, at least!" Chris's eyes shone.

"04, I think. Or possibly 06. Definitely one of those two."

"And when was the last time you saw this vehicle?"

"Two nights ago. I was walking the dog, heading down towards Garthowen shops. It came bumping down the road, over the sleeping policemen. How it doesn't get damage underneath I do not know." She shook her head.

"What time was this?"

"About six o'clock."

Chris held his breath, doubt creeping in. "Ever seen it any earlier than that?"

"Yes, I've seen it around four o'clock, before now."

"I see." He breathed out.

"One time, I was up near the little roundabout, at the top of the road, near Maesyrhandir. And he came racing out of the estate there. That was about three weeks ago."

"Did you recognise the driver?"

"No, I didn't get a clear view. The one time I did, he was wearing a hoody and I didn't see his face."

"How often would you say you'd seen him, altogether?' Jenny asked, also making notes.

"I don't know. Maybe ten or fifteen times. Several times, anyway." Sheena nodded, affirming herself.

"And this car was definitely not a small four-by-four?" Chris rubbed his chin, a frown lining his forehead.

Sheena shook her head. "I don't think it was a four-by-four."

"Thank you, Mrs Moore."

As they closed the gate at number fifty-five, Jenny turned to Chris. "I don't think it's our guy. The model isn't right."

"Yeah, but you heard what she said. She's not good with car models."

"But she also said it probably wasn't a four-by-four."

"I know. It's hard to know what to make of her information, but I think we should feed it back. Colleagues in uniform can keep an eye out for it. I think it was worthwhile talking to her. Let's finish off the final few houses."

Only one other resident had been aware of the car Sheena had seen. They stated that there was more than one car that came down there faster than they should, and they had not looked at the registration.

As they travelled back to the station, Chris shook his head. "Can you believe that? A young boy is killed on their doorstep, and most people just seem so unaware of who is driving down there. If it was me, I'd be observing and taking notes."

Jenny grinned at him. "Yes, Chris, but you *are* a police officer. It's what we do. *And*, I'll bet there aren't that many of the residents that haven't driven a little bit faster than they should, at times. Haven't you?" she asked, one eyebrow raised.

"No." Chris emphatically shook his head. "I stick to the speed limit."

Jenny smiled at him. "You know? I can very well believe it."

22

KENNY CONFRONTS THE KILLER

"You been using my drugs to kill people?" Kenny was only half serious.

"What the fuck you talking about, Kenny?" He could feel every muscle in his body tighten, as though ready to spring. The blood vessels in his temples throbbed. He clenched his fists.

"Cops pulled me in today. Asked me who had GBH around here. Wanted to know if I'd supplied anyone, and saying that someone is dosing people up with GBH and pushing 'em in the river. You've been having a helluva lotta GBH off me."

He breathed in through his nose and out through his mouth. He took his time, voice low. "You tell them that, Kenny?"

"No." Kenny scowled. "What do you take me for? I wouldn't rat on my clients. How would I earn my keep if I shopped 'em all?"

"You tell anyone else, Kenny? Any of your other drug-using pals?"

Kenny took a half-step back. "No. 'Course not."

"Hey, relax. I was just checking." He kept his gaze steadily on the other man.

Kenny looked about him as though suddenly aware he was up here alone with someone who might be a killer.

"Hey, chill. You got the GHB? I'll get the money from my glove compartment."

He saw Kenny's shoulders drop a little.

Kenny gave a nervous laugh. "I got the stuff. I'll go get it from the boot."

He opened his car door and the glove compartment, pulling from it a needle and syringe and a vial of GHB. He filled the syringe, replaced the needle cap and pocketed it. Grabbing the envelope with the money, he crossed over to the trunk of the other man's car.

"You got it, Kenny?"

"Yeah, here - ow!"

He had plunged the syringe into Kenny's thigh, pushing as much of the contents into him as fast as he could.

"What the fuck!" The shock on Kenny's face became a look of horror, as realisation dawned. Kenny began to back away. He tried to get around to his driver's door but was blocked.

"Nowhere to run, Kenny. You might as well give in."

Kenny's legs went from under him. "No...no, please."

"Feeling a little woozy, Kenny?"

Kenny's eyes rolled.

He reached into his jacket pockets and placed on leather gloves. He moved round to the boot of Kenny's car and removed the small drugs stash and money. He came back and kneeled next to Kenny. "You won't be needing this." He showed the near-unconscious man the money, before taking it to his own car and stashing it under the seat.

When he was sure that Kenny was out cold, he grabbed him and threw him over his shoulder in a fireman's lift, placing him in the back of his car. His heart pounded from the risk he was taking. Small, admittedly. Very few people came up here at this time of night. Still, two cars, parked as they were, would draw attention.

He climbed into his front seat, fired up the engine and drove off back the way he had come.

23

PROGRESS

Yvonne strode into the main CID office, straight up to where Chris and Jenny had been waiting for her.

"Hey, you two." She gave them a broad smile. "I hear you've got something for me."

Chris looked at Jenny. "Go on, you tell her."

Jenny flicked through the notes in her pad. "We went back to Garthowen, and spoke to a Sheena Moore. She lives about half-way up the street, opposite the school. She told us about a car that has been driven at speed, a few times, through the twenty-mile-an-hour zone along Plantation Lane."

"Alright." Yvonne perched on the edge of the desk. "Did she know the registration?"

"We got a partial. She thinks it was possibly a Nissan Micra and that the reg was either 04 or 06."

Yvonne tapped her pen on her chin. "That's good work, guys. Very good work. So, it was possibly a Nissan Micra. Problem is, our perp was said to be driving a small, silver four-by-four when he hit Callum."

"That's right," Chris concurred, "but the car was only seen at a distance. And that was by young witnesses, *and* Sheena Moore stated that she wasn't too good with recognising the make and model of cars. So, she could potentially be wrong about it being a Micra. Either she, or the witnesses, could be wrong, and they could be talking about the same car."

"Uh huh. How sure was she that it was one of those two years?"

"Very."

"Okay, well, run some vehicle checks on 04 and 06 silver Nissan Micras in the area and we'll expand it to look at 04 and 06 four-by-fours and see where we get. I know that will take some slog, but you could be onto something and, to be honest, we're desperate for new leads and to move this case forward. Speak to the child witnesses again. Find out if the car they saw could have been a Micra."

"Will do."

"Very good work," Yvonne repeated. "I'll go make the coffees."

"Ma'am?" Chris called after her.

She turned.

"Thanks."

"No, thank *you*."

24

BOUND

W hen Kenny woke up, it took him a several seconds to realise he couldn't move. He was laid out on what looked like a hospital bed and was completely restrained. His head throbbed, and the objects around the room blurred, as he tried desperately to focus his eyes. Opposite, he thought he could make out an open laptop on a desk. There appeared to be a stairwell leading down and the ceiling above him sloped, as though he was at the top of a house.

The room contained various bric-a-brac, strewn around, including old vinyl albums and a few dusty books. He was covered by a white sheet. He called out, intermittently, but there was no answer. In between times, he sobbed, tears and sweat soaking into the sheet. He wasn't hot, he was afraid. He was very afraid.

He heard the door slam shut. It was loud. He was meant to hear it. He pulled against his restraints but there was no give. He'd never felt this scared in his life. And his life flashed in front of him, as he heard footsteps on the stairs. His mother telling him to stay away from drugs. Why hadn't he listened to her instead of always wanting to make that quick buck?

"Why, Kenny..." His would-be torturer had an evil grin. "So good of you to wait around for me."

"You're a sick bastard!" Kenny spat the words, surprised at his own defiance. He whimpered, however, when the other man moved closer.

"Come again? I didn't quite hear that, Kenny."

Kenny shook his head, sweat dripping from his brow.

"You know, Kenny, when a body is at the bottom of a fast running river, it can sometimes bump along the bottom. Your head hangs down low, you're kind of bent over in the water. Injuries can happen to the face... like maybe torn lips and shredded nose. The loss of a few teeth. It can be hard for the pathologist to know whether the injuries occurred before or after death."

Kenny thought he had never seen such an evil sneer in all his life. "You wouldn't. Come on, you wouldn't... Why are you doing this?"

"Because I can? Because I can't afford you blabbing your mouth off to the police?"

"I wouldn't. You know I wouldn't do that." Kenny's eyes were wide. Pleading.

"You know, I'd love to believe that. But, I don't."

"I already told them." Kenny changed tack. "They could be here any minute."

The other man paused.

Kenny prayed inside his head.

"Kenny, if you had told the police about me, they'd be here already. You've been trussed up like a chicken for more than six hours. If the police thought I was killing people, they wouldn't leave it this long to haul me in. But, nice try." He pulled out a small, plastic bottle of water and offered it to Kenny's mouth. "Come on, Kenny, drink up. I can't have you dying on me before I've had some fun."

25

A QUIET TABLE

The excitement of the day over, Chris helped Jenny on with her coat.

She smiled demurely at him. "Thank you. It's been a good day, hasn't it?"

"I think we aced it." Chris grinned. "Listen, how about we go for a drink at the bar tonight?" He was referring to the bar in the Elephant and Castle pub, where they were both rooming whilst on secondment.

Jenny smiled. "You know what? A gin and tonic is exactly what I need."

A short car drive later, they entered the Elephant, glancing up at a TV screen on the wall in the corner, where a football match was in progress.

Jenny looked at Chris who shook his head. "I don't really watch it." He grinned. "Come on, we'll sit over there.

He chose a table by the wall, not too far from the bar. Jenny was grateful.

It was still early evening and the pub was quiet. One lone punter sat at the bar, his back to them, hunched over as though deep in thought. Once Jenny was seated, Chris headed over, standing next to the hunched man. He ordered a gin and tonic and pint of lager.

"Quiet in here, isn't it?" He directed this at the figure who appeared to come out of some deep reverie.

He sat bolt upright, turning to take in the young PC. There was an awkward couple of seconds, before he answered."It's usually pretty quiet in here at this time."

Chris nodded. "I had noticed." He flicked his head in the direction of the stairs. "I'm staying here for a few weeks."

"You that young police officer?" The darkly-dressed man looked him up and down.

Chris raised his eyebrows.

The other man laughed. "Hey, don't come over all suspicious on me. I'm not following you. I was talking to the lass behind the bar last night. I think she might have taken a shine to you." He winked.

Chris relaxed and laughed back. "Oh." He coloured. "I hadn't noticed."

"Anyway," the other man continued, "your secret's safe with me. I'm not going to tell anyone."

"Thank you." Chris nodded to him, as he paid for the drinks. "Not everybody likes police officers."

The other man nodded and Chris left the bar, carrying the drinks back to where Jenny sat waiting.

"Just what I need," she said, by way of thank you.

Chris smiled widely. He liked her. She had a quiet, gentle way about her. He found himself mentally comparing her to his ex-partner, the mother of his daughter. He decided there was no comparison.

"Penny for them?" Jenny asked, taking the first sip of her drink.

"Oh, I was just thinking about my daughter," he answered. "Wondering how she is. I tried ringing her mother last night but she didn't answer." He sighed. "She does that sometimes."

Jenny placed a hand on his. "Try again tonight. Maybe she was just busy."

He nodded, appreciating the touch. He looked down at Jenny's hand.

Jenny cleared her throat and let go. Chris's hand felt cold at the removal.

"Do you mind if I join you?" The figure from the bar stood next to their table. Chris hadn't noticed him approach. He appeared taller than Chris had imagined, and dressed in back, apart from a white shirt underneath his thin, black jumper. Chris wondered if the man had been to a funeral. He didn't really want him to join them but, before he could say anything, Jenny took the decision out of his hands.

"Of course, you can join us." She gave the man a knowing smile, as though a part of her felt sorry for him being on his own. Chris was struck by the tenderness in it.

"I couldn't help overhearing that you miss your daughter," the intruder offered, drawing up a seat.

Chris sighed. "I do. I don't see her nearly enough and her health isn't good."

"I have a daughter. She's all grown up and at college," the other man offered. "I know what it's like to miss them and wish they'd call more often."

Chris nodded. The three of them continued in conversation, until Jenny indicated that she needed to leave.

"I need a shower, and then it's food and an early night for me."

"Me too." Chris pushed his seat back. "I'm sorry," he said

to the gentleman. "We only came here for one drink. It was nice meeting you though."

As when they first met, the other man took a good couple of seconds before replying, all the while looking at Chris's face. "Likewise," was all he said.

26

KENNY'S DEATH

He couldn't scream anymore. When his mouth opened, nothing of any power came out. He was bleeding from his mouth and nose and, along with piercing pain, could taste the slimy mix of blood and mucous making its way down his face. It made him vomit. His torturer had gone 'for a break'. If he had had the means to kill himself, Kenny would have done it. He just couldn't take any more.

When his torturer came back, Kenny steeled himself for the end. He was sure it was coming.

"You see this, Kenny? It's river water. You gotta breath this in. That way, you'll have all the right things in your lungs when they cut you open."

Kenny spat blood and snot in his torturer's face.

The other man wiped it away, tight-lipped. "What, you want some more? Haven't you had enough pain, Kenny? You want more suffering?"

Kenny was unable to do more than shake his head.

As the bag was placed on his head and the bed was tilted back, Kenny tried one last time to fight his bindings. To no avail.

THE QUIET AFTERNOON was pierced by high-pitch sirens of just about every variety. Yvonne stopped what she was doing and ran to the window. A number of uniformed officers were running towards their vehicles in the car park below.

"What's going on?" Dewi joined her at the window.

"I don't know. Ring down to the desk, would you? And find out."

Dewi left her watching, rubbing her chin.

When he came back, he was wide-eyed. "It's another body, ma'am. Another body found in the river. It's in fairly shallow water, near the rapids."

Yvonne closed her eyes, repeating the word, "no," in her mind.

"Ma'am?"

The DI cleared her throat. "Come on." She grabbed her jacket. "We'd better get down there. I want to see the scene when it's fresh. If this is a serial killer, we're letting everyone down. We've got to stop him."

Dewi nodded. "Come on, let's go."

THOUGH IT WAS ONLY MID-AFTERNOON, the sky had darkened considerably. Before they reached the scene, the heavens opened. They had chosen to walk the half-mile to where the body was found. Yvonne did not have a hood on her summer mac, and within minutes her hair was soaked and clinging to her neck. Beads of water dripped from her fringe to her cheeks and nose.

Dewi stepped forward, gallantly holding his jacket over her head.

She smiled appreciatively, but waved it away. "Please put your coat on, Dewi. You'll catch your death."

"I knew we should have taken the car." He grinned.

She nodded, though she could barely hear him. It had been her idea to walk. She had wanted the chance to visually scan the trees along the river path. Looking for numerals. She hadn't seen any.

The scene was hectic. SOCO, scurrying about trying to protect evidence; uniform busy interviewing those who had found the body and creating the cordon; the SAR team, here to recover the body; the photographer, trying to get meaningful shots; and her and Dewi, trying to figure out what the hell was going on.

"I'm sorry, ma'am, I can't let you go any further." A white-plastic, suited arm had shot out to hold her back.

"We're CID." She looked the young SOCO in the eyes. He looked about eighteen.

"I know, ma'am. This one is a suspicious death. I'm preserving evidence." He smiled apologetically.

"It's okay." She nodded towards where the SAR team were working, hauling the body up into the dinghy. "What was suspicious about it?" She wiped water off her forehead with a hanky from her pocket.

"Apparently, there's damage to the face and hands."

"What?" Her eyes narrowed. "How do we know that already?"

The SOCO pointed over to where a couple were being interviewed beneath a large oak. "The guy who found the body waded out to it. He thought he was carrying out a rescue. Except, when he got there, the victim was clearly dead. He said the nose and mouth were injured."

"How do *you* know that?" Yvonne asked, genuinely surprised.

The SOCO pulled a face. "Er, that's what he told you guys when he phoned in. Didn't he?"

"Oh, right. I don't know. I didn't take the call." She

looked back towards the body. What had been a red jacket and blue pants moving intermittently in the water was now a lifeless body bag in a red SAR dinghy. "Was it a male or a female? I thought I saw long hair. I don't suppose they described the injury?"

"Sorry, I've got to get on." He left them to get on with it.

The ambulance was parked, waiting to take the body to the mortuary. Yvonne walked over to it, waiting for the body to be hauled out of the dinghy and over to them.

Once more, she admired the respectful way the SAR team dealt with the victim. The good guys.

As they slowly approached the ambulance, she stepped forward, holding up her badge. "May I see the victim's face?"

"Let her look." She recognised Carwyn's voice, before she spotted him at the rear.

She nodded her thanks.

They laid the body bag on the ground and the front team member slowly unzipped the top, just enough to get a view of the head.

Yvonne drew in a sharp breath. "Kenny?" She put a hand to her forehead, her face screwed up in disbelief. "It looks like Kenny Walters, one of our local drug dealers. How on earth did he end up here?"

She had recognised him from the scar on the side of his face, his long hair and heavy eyebrows. Most of his nose was gone, as his lips and several teeth. She had a feeling he'd been tortured.

Dewi came up on her shoulder. "Oh." He pursed his lips. "That's Kenny Walters. Or, what's left of him."

"We interviewed him only a few days ago, Dewi. Is this our killer making sure he doesn't talk?"

"Don't jump to conclusions." The silent approach of

Roger Hanson made her jump. He pulled back the hood on his white, plastic suit so he could better talk to her.

"But, it *does* look like foul-play, here. Looks like he was tortured."

"That's what I mean." Roger shook his head. "Looks can be deceiving. The body has bumped around the rapids. It's been over a lot of rock. The river's still high, and fast-moving. That kind of force over rock can damage facial features and be a bit misleading. I'm not ruling out foul-play, but it could just as easily be naturally-occurring damage."

"I see." The DI pursed her lips. "Then, I guess I'd better wait until you've finished the autopsy."

"Would be the best idea." Hanson smiled, his grey-curls becoming darker with the soaking from the rain. "I'll let you know as soon as I possibly can."

27

KENNY WASN'T DRUNK

Yvonne was seated in the coffee area, a mug of hot chocolate clutched in her hands and a towel around her head. She let the heat soak through her hands and up her arms, pressing the mug to her chest, as though to warm her heart.

Dewi brought his coffee over. "Penny for them?" He tilted his head, to get a look at the DI's face, as she was bent over towards her drink.

"I know we still haven't had a verdict from the pathologist, but I can't help thinking that Kenny may have been murdered to shut him up." She sat up straight, looking her sergeant in the eye. "Someone didn't want him talking to us. Someone made sure he wouldn't."

Dewi nodded. "I'm inclined to agree." He leaned back in his chair, arms folded. "Kenny didn't drink."

"What? Do you mean he didn't drink alcohol?"

"Not at all. I've always known him as being allergic to it. He wouldn't touch it. Apparently, he was hospitalised when he was seventeen due to a bad reaction. So, whatever caused him to end up in the river, you can bet your bottom dollar it *wasn't* alcohol."

IN THE END, they had to wait several days for Hanson's full assessment. It had rested on the toxicology report.

Yvonne's hands shook, as she picked up her mobile, and saw the call was from him.

"Hi, Roger. Do you have an answer for us?" she paced the floor.

"I do."

"That's great." She exhaled a massive puff of air.

"You may not like it-"

"Try me."

"Death by drowning."

"Okay, but was foul-play involved?" She struggled to hide her exasperation.

"I can't be sure."

"What do you mean, you can't be sure?"

"We found a fairly large amount of GHB in his blood, meaning he took it shortly before his death. I found a high concentration of it in his thigh muscle, around a puncture wound made by a needle."

"Right, so someone injected him with it?"

"Yes, himself."

"Kenny injected himself with GHB? Why would he have done that?" She frowned at the phone.

"We found the used syringe in his jacket pocket. The thigh was on his right-hand-side and the jacket pocket also on his right-hand-side."

"Are you telling me you think he injected himself with GHB and then fell or jumped in the river?"

"It seems that way, yes."

"What about the facial injuries?"

"Well, they were pretty much congruent with having bumped along the river bed, as the water was fast-flowing. It's very possible they sustained that damage on the rocks. Except-"

"Except, what? Spit it out, for goodness' sake."

"The nose damage had a straighter edge than I would have expected. There was some tearing, but it was minimal in comparison to the amount of damage."

"Could the nose have been cut off with a knife?"

"If it was, it was a very blunt knife... or a blunt pair of scissors. Like I say, there *was* tear-damage. I can't say, definitively, whether the damage was naturally-occurring or man-made. I mean, I can't rule out a sharp bit of rock, like slate, causing the damage."

The DI sighed heavily, her shoulders hunched, appeared as though she had aged a few years in just a few moments.

"I'm sorry, I can't give you more than that." Hanson sighed and the DI relented.

"I'm sorry, too. I expect an awful lot of you, I know. It's just that I really suspected that Kenny was killed because we talked to him. I was convinced we had a killer running scared. That's all."

"Well, you still may have. I just can't confirm it one way or another."

"Alright. Well, thank you anyway, Roger. You are always a great help to us."

"ARE YOU OKAY?" Dewi's eyes were full of concern.

"Yes, I'm fine, Dewi. I was just hoping for more. Hanson thinks Kenny probably injected himself with GHB."

"The DCI has asked to see the report." Dewi scratched his head. "This isn't going to help your case to get the extra resources you need."

"I'll speak to the DCI. In the meantime, we need to take stock - look at everything we have and ask ourselves, honestly, what we think is going on. I'll be the first to admit if I have been jumping off the deep end and looking for a serial killer where none exists. But, I do think we need to delve a little deeper into Kenny's life. Find out who he really was and what he got up to. Ask Jones and Clayton to do some digging."

"Will do, ma'am."

28

BUDGETS

"Come in." DCI LLewellyn smiled warmly at her, as she entered his office. That gave her hope.

"Thank you, sir. I came to ask you what you make of the pathologist's report into Kenny Walter's death." She held her breath.

"It's hard to say, Yvonne. I think I know what you're thinking, but this is looking like a suicide to me."

"Why would Kenny commit suicide? He didn't come across as someone who cared that deeply about stuff going on in his life. We have nothing to suggest he was suicidal."

"You've talked to his family, then?"

Yvonne looked down at her shoes. "Not yet. That is next on my to-do list. However, we did talk to him last week and he did not come across as suicidal or even mildly depressed."

"You thought he may have been the dealer who supplied the GHB that killed William Henkel, right?"

"Well, yes. I thought, perhaps, he may have dealt it to William's killer."

"What if he dealt it direct to William? William accidentally takes too much, gets lost and falls in the river. Kenny guilt trips over that and decides to top himself. It happens."

Yvonne grimaced and shook her head. "You don't really think that, do you?"

The DCI leaned back in his chair, placing both hands behind his head. "It's an open verdict, Yvonne. That scenario would be as likely as anything else. But, since the pathologist thinks Kenny injected himself in the thigh, I'd say there's more than a slight chance that he committed suicide. I mean, it's possible that more of the recent river deaths have been the result of drugs dealt by Kenny. GHB leaves the body very quickly, as you know. Maybe the guilt became too much."

Yvonne's enlarged pupils made her eyes look black. She placed her hands firmly on her hips. "You mean the budget's tight and wrapping everything up in a neat little bow is going to save money and earn you a slap on the back from the commissioner."

"Yvonne. What the hell...?"

"I'm sorry. That was uncalled for. I just... I just have a bad feeling about this and I don't want more young men to die because we didn't give this the time, attention and manpower it deserves. If we get this wrong..."

"It'll be on my head, not yours."

Yvonne swallowed hard, but the lump was still in her throat. She turned wistful eyes towards the window. "I'll stand the team down for the river deaths."

The DCI's face relaxed as he nodded. "Get your focus back on the hit-and-run."

"We are making headway with that-"

"Good. I want an interim report on my desk by the end of the week."

And that was that. Yvonne bit her lip on the way out of

his office. Self-doubt clouded her thoughts. Maybe the DCI was right and she had got this wrong from the beginning. When she analysed it, she had had little more than gut instinct and that was no kind of evidence. Perhaps, this was the fall-out from having dealt with so many serial killers. She was seeing them everywhere.

She needed Tasha.

29

LIFE OF A DEALER

Yvonne and Dewi parked their unmarked car in the street off a cul-de-sac in Trehafren. They were due to see Kenny Walters' parents, Jim and Mary. They were here to give them some sort of closure. In reality, this could have been done by victim liaison, but the DCI had already given his permission, and Yvonne was secretly hoping that they would know something. Some small detail that would blow the case wide open.

There were no flowers in the front garden and the grass was around two feet high. An old wheel, a bicycle frame and an upturned bird bath lay where they had fallen. Passers-by had used the Walters' garden as a bin, depositing crisp packets, empty plastic bottles and sweet packets.

Dewi rang the doorbell.

The door was opened by Kenny's mum. She wiped tears away from swollen eyes as she led them through the narrow hallway into the kitchen. She dragged two stools out for the officers to sit.

Her greying hair was tied up in a simple ponytail, from which several tendrils had worked loose. She wore no make up and appeared as pale as the cream tiles above the kitchen counter.

"I'll go get Jim." Mary left them alone.

When she reappeared, Jim followed closely behind, relying heavily on a walking cane, his steps slow and painful.

"Jim's back is crumbling," Mary said by way of explanation. "He needs help to do most things." She aided her husband into a custom-made chair, in the front room, before showing the officers to a two-seater sofa near the door, overlooking the garden.

Jim said nothing, but stared first at Yvonne, and then Dewi, waiting for either to talk.

"Thank you for seeing us." Yvonne kept her voice soft and low. "Firstly, I have to tell you how sorry I am for your loss."

Jim grunted. Mary glanced at him and then back to the detectives, and nodded.

The DI continued. "Kenny was well-known about town and had a lot of friends."

"They said it was suicide," Mary blurted out. "Suicide. My Kenny. He enjoyed life. Why would he commit suicide?" She cried, painful sobs wracking her body. She could barely get the following words out. "He...h...he was due to come for Sunday roast, the...the...day after he disappeared. He told me not to forget his giant Y...Yorkshires. He told me that the Saturday afternoon and they reckon he killed himself later that day. I...I don't believe it." She sat back, appearing exhausted from the effort.

Yvonne nodded. "I have to say, I was very surprised when I heard the news, Mrs Walters. Kenny was so full of life."

"You lot kept stopping him." Jim scowled at her. "Always

searching him in the street. Always coming round 'ere to find out where he was."

Yvonne forced herself to look away from his big hands to Jim's bitter expression, her own soft, her eyes large and glistening.

"Kenny was always polite to me," Dewi offered. "I talked to him, a few times. I didn't search him, but, you have to admit, he was no angel."

Yvonne flicked Dewi a look, clearing her throat. "Kenny enjoyed life to the full," she said. "We obviously didn't approve of everything he did, but he was a trier. No-one can take that away from him."

"We didn't have much, when he was growing up." Mary's sobs had quietened down, allowing her to properly get her words out. "When he was little, he'd set up a table outside with a little pot and put all his old toys, and anything his friends no longer wanted, up for sale. Making pennies for sweets. Pennies to save up for something he wanted. He'd run errands for people. Take their post. Do some gardening. Anything to earn a bit."

"He was bullied rotten in school." Jim's eyes still held a mild accusation. "He'd come home bruised and cut, clothes ripped. Where were the authorities then? When I went to the school, they'd tell us it was six of one and half-a-dozen of the other." He took a deep, painful breath. "And now, you tell us he committed suicide. Where's the justice?"

"I understand your hurt and frustration." Yvonne sighed. "There was just nothing to suggest foul-play and certainly no evidence of any other hand in your son's death."

Jim snorted his disgust. "Who commits suicide by injecting themselves with drugs and then throwing themselves in a cold, dirty river? Who? If he wanted to commit suicide, he'd have just used the drugs. Painkillers and alcohol would have been better, surely."

"Someone else injected him and someone else pushed him in the river." Mary appeared emboldened. That pusher-bloke in the papers. People are saying there's a killer who's pushing young men in the river. Maybe that's who killed our Kenny?"

Yvonne rubbed her chin, before taking out her notebook and pen. "Alright, Jim...Mary, tells us about your last few days with Kenny. What did he say about where he was going and who he was seeing? I'm not saying I agree that he was murdered, but I'm prepared to look into it. Did he confide in you about being afraid of anyone?"

Mary shook her head. "He didn't say he was afraid of anyone. Kenny felt he could handle himself in most situations."

"What did he say to you about that that Saturday night? Did he tell you where he was going?"

"He said he was meeting someone. He said he'd buy us the new TV he'd been promising, if the meeting went well."

"Did he say who he was meeting?"

"No." Mary shook her head. "But he said it was important and he couldn't miss it."

"What about the place? Did he say *where* he was meeting someone?"

"He didn't, but..."

"Go on," Yvonne prompted.

"He asked me where his big jacket was. He said it'd be windy up there."

"And he didn't say where 'up there' was?"

"No."

"Okay. Well, that's something, anyway. Sounds like he was meeting someone out of town."

"That's the impression I got."

"Did he say how long he'd be gone?"

"He said he'd be no more than a couple of hours."

"So, couldn't have been that far away."

"No."

"Okay, well, you've been very helpful." Yvonne looked from Mary to Jim and back again.

"Promise us you'll look into it?" Mary's eyes pleaded.

"I will. I promise."

As they left the Walters' home, Yvonne turned to her sergeant. "Dewi, where's the most likely place you might go to do a big drug deal, if you were going out of town and were expecting it to be windy?"

"Honestly?"

"Yes."

"Well, probably a few places, but the Dolfor Moors comes to mind."

"The Dolfor Moors?"

"There's minor road with no markings that goes over the top of the hills between Dolfor and Llanbadarn Fynydd. It runs for about ten miles through the wilderness. Only the sheep up there. The odd motorist uses it as a shortcut, but it's not a great road. Pretty secluded, though. A good place for a meeting if you want it well away from people."

"And, well away from CCTV cameras." Yvonne nodded. "Come on, we're going up there."

MEETING PLACE

They Parked their car on a dry piece of ground, just off the narrow farmer's road. As they got out, Yvonne could see modern windmills off to her right, and to her left and right, fields of highly-grazed grass. "I see what you mean about desolate," she said to Dewi, as he joined her.

"Imagine it at dusk or after dark. You're right about it being a pretty ideal spot to carry out a deal, if you didn't want to be observed." Dewi scanned the horizon.

"So, where would they have parked?"

"Well, that's the problem. They could have agreed to meet up any where along this stretch, or even further along. But, after dark? You're probably better off using a passing-point to park up. Otherwise, you risk getting your wheels stuck in the ditches."

Yvonne nodded.

"There's a passing point just down there." Dewi pointed at the place where the road widened due to a tiny lay-by. "Could fit two cars parked up, there."

"Let's go check it out."

They walked the few hundred yards to the passing-place.

Dewi pointed to the fresh tyre-tracks in the dirt. "Looks like someone's been here, recently."

Yvonne crouched. "There's few different tracks. You got a decent camera on your phone?" She took out her mobile and took several shots from various angles.

"Want me to take some, too?" Dewi pulled out his mobile.

"If you can. Mine should be usable, but it'll make sure that lab have something they can work with. We can compare these tracks with..." Yvonne scratched her head, frowning. "Kenny's car."

"Ma'am?"

"I don't remember hearing anything about his car."

"It's probably at his parents' house."

"What does he drive?"

"Er, it's a silver Suzuki, I think. Uniform could tell us. What are you thinking?"

"That, if he drove up here to do a drug deal and he was taken from here, then the perpetrator would have had to do something with Kenny's car. Find the car, we find out what happened to Kenny."

"I'll get on it as soon as we get back."

Yvonne attempted to skim a stone across the water. It hit with a 'plump' and sank. She shrugged her shoulders. "That says it all." She gave a short, self-deprecating laugh.

Tasha's stone skimmed the surface four times before sinking.

"You been practising?" The DI raised an eyebrow, an accusing smile softening her face.

"Just naturally talented." Tasha giggled.

Yvonne turned her gaze back to the water. The sea was calmer than she'd seen it in a while. The main bay at Aberystwyth had been full of students and families enjoying the sea and promenade. The two women had chosen to make their way around the rock pools and stony beach at the bottom of Constitution Hill. A Saturday away from it all.

"Are you going to tell me what's eating you? You've barely said a word for an hour." Tasha walked up to her friend and, placing a hand under her chin, tilted her head up, to get eye contact with her. "I know that look. That's the despondent look that comes over you when you're at your wits' end with a case. Is this the river murders? Is that case eating you up?"

"They're not murders, Tasha. They're most likely misadventures." The DI sighed. "And, if they are murders, the killers are drink and drugs. Lethal combination."

"Oh." Tasha's screwed-up face signalled her confusion. "What about all those doubts? All those things that didn't add up?" Tasha grabbed another flat stone and skimmed it. This time it bounced only once, at an angle, before sinking.

"I think I was probably making more of things than was warranted." Yvonne found a large, flat-ish rock and seated herself on it, staring down at her walking boots.

Tasha sat on the small shale, next to her. "So, the chalk numerals, the frightened voicemail, the lads wandering in places they didn't need to be, and lack of injury of one victim who had supposedly fallen down onto large boulders, were nothing to be concerned over?"

Yvonne looked up at her friend, eyes flicking from side-to-side, studying her face. "You see? You saying it like that, gives me that feeling all over again. Like there's more to this. But I'm the only one in my station who really thinks so." She hesitated. "Well, I've got Dewi's support, but I think I led him into believing there was more to it. You, too."

"Listen." Tasha shook her head. "You didn't lead me into anything. You informed me of the facts you'd observed, some of which I was able to see for myself, and I drew the same conclusions."

"You did? Really?"

"Hey, come on. I'm a grown woman and a psychologist. I think I am more than capable of making my own mind up, Yvonne." Tasha frowned.

"I know." The DI shook her head and put a hand on Tasha's arm. "If only we had something more clear-cut. Something concrete. Something which shouted murder from the rooftops. Instead, it's like I've been investigating shadows. One minute I see a killer, the next it's a horrible accident."

"Water makes everything more difficult, you know that. For example, there was a case a few years back, in the US. A young lad was thought to have accidentally drowned after a night out. It was nearly two years later that the accidental drowning was changed to murder. They found his own hair clutched in his hand, after someone had spotted it in evidence photographs. They figured that he must have been trying to grab at someone else's hands, whilst that person was holding his head under the water. Instead, he grabbed his own hair. Like you said to me, deaths on land can be ring-fenced and properly studied, forensically. When a person dies in water, the body will likely have changed position; trace evidence will have been washed away and injuries created or disguised - blood from gashes washed away. It's a forensic nightmare."

"You're right about that." Yvonne sighed.

"But, I know you." Tasha moved around to the front of Yvonne's rock, looking up into her friend's eyes. "I know your instincts are sound. I've also seen enough, myself, to think that if we don't investigate these deaths, we may be doing a great disservice to the friends and relatives of the deceased. And we may seal the fate of future victims."

"The DCI thinks there's not enough to go on."

"The DCI has one eye on his budget and the commissioner breathing down his neck."

Yvonne nodded.

"Let me profile him, this putative killer. Let me give him a shape. A form. Even if you can't officially investigate, it'll be something for you to look out for. And he won't stop. Serial killers never stop. They have to *be* stopped. In fact, if he knows you've ceased looking for him, he may even up his game. The guy who left those Roman numerals wants notoriety, whether he's aware of it or not."

"Do it." Yvonne nodded, her eyes earnest. "Put a profile together and I'll share it with Dewi. If we have a suspect who fits, I'll go again to the DCI."

31

KILLER TAKES AN INTEREST IN
THE CASE

'*an found in river thought to have taken his own life.*'

M

He read the headline with disdain, cursing loudly as he continued down the column.

Kenny Walters, 26, died after overdosing on the illicit drug GHB and falling in the river near Newtown in Powys.

Ideas of The Pusher having come to Mid-Wales have once-and-for-all been dispelled by DCI Christopher Llewellyn. 'It is only natural for people to be concerned when several bodies are found in the river in one year. However, I can reassure the community that this is not the work of some diabolical killer, but a combination of young men consuming too much alcohol and/or drugs and falling into a river, which has been higher than normal this summer and fast-flowing. A coming together of a disastrous mix of unfortunate circumstances.'

He skimmed several paragraphs.

The DCI finished by saying, 'I would warn any would-be revellers to take care around our river paths. The water should be respected at all times.'

HE KICKED at the table leg, as he leaned back in his chair. On the one hand, they'd fallen for it hook, line and sinker. He should feel proud of setting everything up so well. But, where was the confusion? Where was the copper with some nouse, who would read the numbers he left on the trees and suspect there was more to it. Why wasn't he in the middle of a mental chess game? Why was this all becoming too easy? And, why were the community so ready to give up on their fears that a serial killer was running amok amongst their young?

He pulled a large piece of chalk from his drawer. Time to leave the number five and then mix things up a bit.

32

PERMISSION FOR LEAVE

Yvonne climbed the stairs two-by-two, her brain still mulling over the river deaths, despite her having little time to devote to them. She was rubbing her forehead, as she entered CID and almost collided with Chris Halliwell, who appeared to be hovering near her office.

"Are you okay?" She frowned, wanting not to be irritated, but irritated nonetheless.

"Ma'am." He cleared his throat. "Can I have a word?"

"Er..." She opened the door, signalling for him to go inside. "Yes, of course. Go ahead. What can I do?"

"I'm so sorry, I've come to request leave."

"Leave?" She ran her eyes over his loosened tie, his hand-combed hair and the sweat on his upper lip. "It's very short notice. Is everything alright? Has something happened?"

"It's my daughter. She's been taken into hospital with a severe asthma attack. I'd really like to be with her if at all possible."

"Oh God, I'm so sorry." She rushed over to him, placing

a hand on each arm. "Of course, you can have as much leave as you need. Which hospital is she in?"

"She's in the Royal Shrewsbury, ma'am. Her mother is with her, but I need to be there. We nearly lost her, previously."

Yvonne nodded. "I'll speak to the DCI and let PC Hadley know you'll be away a while."

"Thank you. I did speak to Jenny, to let her know the situation. We are in the middle of chasing up Nissan Micras and small four-by-fours, for the hit-and-run. I feel bad about leaving her to it."

"Jenny's a big girl. I'm sure she'll be just fine. Anyway, I'm sure I can free up Callum or Dai, to help her out. You just concentrate on your girl and on getting her well again." She gave him a warm smile. "Is there anything you need from us?"

He shook his head. I'll be driving straight there, as soon as I've got a bag together from home. I'll fill in a leave request form."

"Don't worry about it, Chris, fill it in when you get back. The only thing I would ask..." She handed him her card. "Is that you call me and let me know how your little girl is doing."

He smiled, relaxing his features. "I will, ma'am." He dashed out of her office and down the stairs.

PC HALLIWELL CLIMBED into his Mini, in the station car park, unaware that he was being observed. He continued unaware, as the tailing vehicle made a left into Park Street and on, following him to the Elephant and Castle public house, where Chris had his temporary accommodation. The young PC parked his vehicle in a small car park, to the left-hand-side of the pub, and ran inside to get his stuff.

His stalker, dressed in black, hood up, followed the shadows, along the wall separating the car park from the river path below. He took a rag out of his pocket and stuffed it into the exhaust of the Mini, returning to his car, to wait.

He'd gleaned all he could from the conversation at the pub, two weeks before. Had been told all about Chris's daughter and her fight with illnesses. He'd been concocting his plan ever since. The most difficult part had been tackling the inevitable phone call Chris would want to make to his child's mother. Aping a consultant over the phone was easy, but persuading a father not to contact the mother of his sick child was a little more tricky. He'd achieved it by saying that she never left her daughter's bedside on ICU, and that her mobile phone had to be switched off so that it didn't interfere with the equipment. Hence the reason he, the doctor, was calling. The policeman had been surprisingly easy to convince.

He didn't have to wait long: about the time it took for a shower. Chris Halliwell came running back to the car park and straight to his vehicle. He had a tiny bit of trouble starting it, but got it running fine. It would be a while down the road, when it was getting dark, before the engine trouble would really kick in. It would require some improvisation, but improvisation was something he was very good at.

"HEY, can I help you? You got engine trouble?" He walked over to where Chris was holding a torch under his bonnet.

Chris bumped his head, as he pulled back. "Ouch. Ooh, that hurt. Er, yes, I've got warning signs on the dash and the engine's sounding a bit off. Thought I'd take a look. It's not a good time.

I'm trying to get to the hospital. Hey..." Chris shone his torch at the other man. "Don't I know you?"

"Wow, you're that young police officer on secondment at Newtown, aren't you?"

"Yes."

"We got talking the other week. Well, I didn't think I'd be meeting you again, out here, like this."

He tutted, shaking his head towards the engine. "Look, if you've got to get to the hospital, you should get going. I tell you what, why don't I tow you to the nearest garage? You can drop your car off in their yard and phone them tomorrow to let them know it's there and to ask them if they can take a look. In the meantime, I can drive you to the hospital. Er, that is, if it's a local hospital?"

"Shrewsbury."

"Wow, no way. I'm going to Shrewsbury. I go there regularly, to visit my mum. I can probably give you a lift back to the garage, in a few days, or whenever you need it." He held his breath. How would he know that PC might be away a few days? He needn't have worried, Chris Halliwell didn't appear to notice.

"That is so kind of you. Listen, I can't thank you enough. You'll have to let me pay you something."

"Hey, it's the least I can do. Who you visiting in hospital?"

"My daughter. She's had a severe asthma attack. She's on a ventilator."

"Right, let's get your vehicle hooked up to mine and I'll tow you to a garage." He smiled to himself. This was too easy.

TASHA'S PROFILE

Tasha banged the knocker on Yvonne's door as hard as she could. If the DI was in the kitchen, she often wouldn't hear the front door.

Yvonne appeared in a large, checkered apron, with floury hands and face.

"What you been up to?" Tasha laughed at the mess her friend was in.

"I'm making stew. I just floured up the beef ready to fry and managed to split the bag of flour. And now, I've just trailed it all through the lounge." Yvonne grimaced. "That wasn't the plan."

"Where's the vacuum cleaner?" Tasha grinned.

Yvonne directed her to a cupboard in the hallway.

"Right. You go back to the kitchen and sort out your beef. I'll get this lot cleaned up. It'll be sorted in no time. Take this with you." Tasha handed her a bottle of red.

Yvonne's smile lit up her face. "Thank you, Tasha. This is why we're mates."

When Tasha had finished vacuuming up the flour, she washed her hands and joined Yvonne in the kitchen. "That smells fantastic," she said of the beef, being fried with garlic and onions.

"Dinner's going to be a couple of hours, I'm afraid." Yvonne apologised.

"No problem." Tasha shook her head. "I cam here early so that I could run my offender profile past you. See what you think and if you'll find it helpful."

Yvonne poured the seared meat into a large pot with the rest of the vegetables and stock, loaded it into the oven, and cleaned herself up. "Right, let's have a look."

Tasha poured two large glasses of the Cabernet Sauvignon and followed Yvonne through to the lounge, so that they could examine the profile.

The DI pulled over a coffee table and spread the paperwork onto it, along with an A4 notepad and pen. "Right, let's have a look at your profile first."

Tasha manoeuvred the pages so that she could read them. "I think this will be a self-assured individual in the age range of thirty-five to fifty years old. Most likely large in stature or, if short in height, they will be muscular - possibly working out at the gym, working the land or involved in otherwise manual work such as building work. They will know the night life in Newtown, and the surrounding area, well. So, they will spend a lot of time either out drinking in town, or else be employed within the night-life scene - perhaps as a bouncer.

"The individual will most likely be charming, able to strike up a conversation with strangers easily. They may be wrestling with gender identity, or with their sexuality. I think it's likely they own property in the area, or else have access to property or land, where they will have a shed or lock-up at their disposal. I believe the unsub will have gotten to know his victims before killing them, and has a fetish for water and the act of drowning - most likely gaining sexual satisfaction from the act of drowning, itself, i.e. the specific control given to them by drowning and then reviving their victim numerous times. This unsub will most likely be using water to torture victims prior to their deaths."

"So, you think they're abducting the victims and holding them somewhere?"

"Yes, I do. It's the only way they would be able to have the prolonged control over life and death that they find so stimulating. Yes, they could carry out that controlled drowning-reviving cycle whilst at the river, but the risk of discovery would be that much greater. I rather think that, for the most part, at least, the river is used merely for disposal and as a cover for their crimes."

"We could start investigating lock-ups almost immediately."

"One more thing, this person seeks notoriety. This may be from online peers or from more public places. I had a thought that the chalked numerals may be for some group they are involved with, such as an online water-fetish group. Something of that nature. If it's a more public fame they seek, you can expect them to up their game since the DCI went so public with denouncing 'The Pusher' theory. If this unsub was loving the media attention, he'll do something, imminently, to get it back."

Yvonne stared at the psychologist, the implication dawning on her. "So, someone will die again very soon."

"It's possible, even likely." Tasha nodded.

"My normal response would be to up patrols in the town centre. I don't know if I can arrange that, now we are not officially investigating these deaths." Yvonne pursed her lips.

"What about getting them on some other pretext?"

"Hmm." Yvonne nodded. "I'll think of something."

"So, what about your suspects? Do you have anyone in the frame for these crimes? Someone we can examine against the profile?" Tasha took a mouthful of wine.

Yvonne nodded and reached for her notes, picking them up so she could read them out.

"There are three men I've had concerns about. The first is Rob Davies. He's a student at the college in Newtown. Twenty-two years old, tall, lean and toned. He seems mild-mannered, when sober, but has been described as loud and arrogant when he's had a few drinks. He had a run-in with James, the night James disappeared."

"And James was the first victim?"

"Right. He has access to allotments sheds and green-houses. Doesn't fit the profile in terms of age, though."

"Okay, well, the unsub may *not* fit the profile in every regard. He does tick a few boxes, so we won't rule him out, yet. Who else?"

"Geoff Griffiths. He works as a barman at the Sports-man. I think he also works for other bars, when they are short-staffed. That is, if he's not working at the Sportsman. He's tall, broad and thirty-five years old. A bit gruff, but appears to keep the bar in order and sorts out any trouble on his own. The Sportsman doesn't have security. By all accounts, he keeps himself to himself outside of work. Used to be a maths teacher until he went off on long-term sick leave, and then took offered redundancy two years ago. A pupil at Newtown High School had accused Griffiths of attacking him. He was ultimately found not guilty. The boy was suspected of hurting himself to get Griffiths in trouble, because of a grudge. Griffiths was one of the last people to see both James and Lloyd alive. I am not aware of his having a lock-up but we haven't been to his home. It's something we can check out."

"Sounds like a reasonable candidate." Tasha nodded. "Who's the third on your list?"

"Clive Jones. He's a farmer, well-muscled and of medium height. Forty-five years old. He works outdoors a lot and has a ruddy complexion. He's used to being out and about on the land. He's a bit rough around the edges - got a reputation for being prickly. He dresses up in a shirt and tie to go out in town, every Friday and Saturday night. This coincides with the nights the young men go missing. He had a heated altercation with Lloyd, the night he went missing. There was a stand-off between the two sets of friends."

"Another good candidate. How are you going to check them out? Especially, now the DCI has called you off?"

"I'm investigating a hit-and-run death of a young boy. I'm desperate to get it solved. The parents need closure and Callum needs justice. We're checking out a lot of vehicles in the area. I may be able to link this in with that investigation, somehow."

Tasha nodded. "Good idea."

34

HALLIWELL

Chris Halliwell blinked in the darkness, unsure of where he was. Struggling to focus his eyes, and still coming round, he wondered why he was having difficulty breathing. It didn't take long to realise he was restrained, and the wide band over his chest was what was inhibiting his upper body movement. Was he in hospital?

On attempting to move, he soon realised that it wasn't just his chest that was restrained. He was unable to move any part of his body, aside from his head. His mouth was also, mercifully, free.

He shook his head, trying to remember how he had gotten into this situation. He was in a dark room, but could see a chink of moonlight coming through the curtains of a small window to his left. He was covered in a white sheet and, when the moon was uncovered by clouds, could make out a little of the room and its contents. It appeared to be an attic. Although he could make out vague shapes, he couldn't focus enough to make out what those shapes were. His head swam, and he set it back down, taking as deep a breath as he was able, given the weight of the restraints.

He frowned in the darkness. His car had broken down.

Someone had come to help. His daughter. He needed to get to his daughter.

"Help!" *he called into the darkness.* "Please, help me...somebody?"

The sound of feet on wooden stairs.

"Hello?" *He listened hard, sweat beading on his brow and upper lip. He licked it off, the saltiness strangely comforting.* "Hello?" *he called, again. His heart thudded in his chest and he could no longer hear anything save the blood in his ears.*

A figure appeared in the room. He must have come up from below. Chris blinked in the half-light, trying to make out a face.

"Do you need water?"

He recognised the voice. He pulled against his restraints, the effort tightening his jaw. "I need to see my daughter. I have to get to the hospital."

"There's nothing wrong with your daughter." *The words were delivered coldly matter-of-fact.*

"No. No, you don't understand. She's very ill. She's in the hospital. Please..."

"She's not at the hospital." *He was standing at the foot of the bed.*

"Wait, what? But I had a phone call."

"I called you."

It took a moment to register. "This was a trap?"

"And you fell right into it. How does that feel, PC Halliwell?"

"What do you want with me? I can't tell you anything. We are told stuff on a need-to-know basis. I can't give you inside information on anything."

The dark figure shrugged. "I don't remember asking you for inside information."

"Then, why?" *Chris narrowed his eyes, in an attempt to improve their focus on the figure.*

"Sport."

"Sport? I don't understand."

"I like Watersport. You'll understand when you wake up tomorrow. Your head will be clear and you'll know exactly what is going on."

"I need the toilet." Chris fought against his restraints.

"Then, go."

"What, here?"

"Well, you're not going anywhere else."

"You can't keep me here. It's a serious offence, kidnapping a police officer."

"Good job no-one knows I've kidnapped you then, eh?"

"They'll be looking for me. My DI will-"

"Your DI thinks you're at the hospital, with your daughter. And she's probably sound asleep right now. She's not about to do anything, is she?"

"Look, please..." Chris closed his eyes, laying his head back on the pillow. "Tell me what you want from me."

The figure came closer, holding a small bottle of water to Chris's mouth, for him to drink. "All will become clear, tomorrow."

35

A DAWNING REALISATION

During coffee break, at CID, Yvonne checked her mobile, hoping for a missed call or a text message from Chris Halliwell. There was none. It had been almost forty-eight hours since she had last seen him. She hoped his daughter was alright. She placed her mobile back in her bag.

"Everything okay?" Dewi eyed her, head tilted to one side.

Yvonne sighed. "I'd hoped to hear something from Chris by now...about his daughter. I'm just hoping everything is alright. But, the longer we spend without communication from him, well...I'm just fearing the worst."

"It may not be bad news. He'll be spending time holding his little girl's hand and reassuring her. Contacting us is probably the last thing on his mind. He'll be in touch soon, I'm sure."

She knew this was Dewi's attempt at comforting her and she was grateful to him. But, something in her gut niggled away. Something didn't feel right and she couldn't shake the unease enveloping her.

"Dewi, I'd like to visit Clive Jones again today. Want to come?"

"Sure. What we looking for?"

"Officially? We're looking at his vehicle. Unofficially, I'm hoping to find out his movements, the night Kenny disappeared."

"Right you are, ma'am. I'll drive." He looked down at her shoes. "Probably best change into wellies."

THEY FOUND him mucking one of the cow sheds. Yvonne put a hand on Dewi's arm, to halt him, as they stood near the entrance. She walked over to the nearest metal railings and leaned against them, observing.

Clive Jones was engrossed in his work, throwing down fresh hay in the pens where the calves would later be. He still hadn't noticed their presence. He seemed relaxed.

The DI gave Dewi a nod and then walked forward to greet the farmer.

He appeared startled, as he sensed their presence. "What the? Oh, it's you, again." He went back to his sweeping. "I haven't got time to do this now." He scowled.

"To do what?" Yvonne asked, head tilted to one side.

"Talk to you lot. I suppose you've come about the car in the top field."

She shot a look at Dewi. "What car?"

He looked up from his sweeping, his eyes searching hers, as though suspecting her of trying to trick him.

"The burned-out car in the top field." He hawked deep in the back of his throat, spitting it out to the side.

The DI flinched. "I didn't know there was a burned-out car in the top field. What car is it?"

"I dunno what car it is. It's all burned, like. Looked like a four-by-four. Small."

"Whose is it? Is it yours?"

"Nope."

"Can we see it?"

"Help yourselves."

"When did you find it?"

"Last night. I was up feeding the sheep."

"Was it still alight?"

"No flames, if that's what you mean. But, it was smoking. The fire had finished. If you ask me, someone had poured petrol on it and set it alight."

"Why would they do that?" Yvonne narrowed her eyes at him.

"Joy riders, I guess. Stole a car to get home and burned it to destroy the evidence. It happens. Probably teenagers." He shrugged.

"We've been looking for a small four-by-four, in connection with a hit-and-run death, near the school. You know anything about that?"

"I saw it in the paper. Felt sorry for the kid." He grunted the words, as though they were said grudgingly. Showing emotion was clearly something that Clive Jones was not used to.

"Why didn't you call it in?" Dewi asked.

"I was going to later today. I didn't realise it was urgent. Hell, there was a car burned out and left on my land for years, before. I didn't notice anyone feeling that was urgent. And, nobody wanted to help get it shifted. I don't see the point in telling the police, if they don't do anything about it. No-one bats an eyelid round here. Kids get away with murder." He threw his broom down. "If you wanna see it, I'll take you up there now. We'll take the Landrover."

36

BURNED OUT

There were still small tendrils of smoke drifting up from the wreck, occasionally. As Clive Jones parked up the Land Rover, Yvonne jumped out. Dewi quickly followed.

"They did a good job on this, didn't they?" She could see that the insides were completely burned out, as she moved in closer.

"Smells like accelerants." Dewi placed the tips of his fingers to the metal. "Cold. The fire's been out a while. Looks like a silver Suzuki." Dewi sighed. "O4 reg. This could be the vehicle we've been looking for. Maybe, whoever ran over and killed Callum Jenkins torched the evidence."

"Wait a minute." Yvonne frowned. "Didn't you say that Kenny Walters drove a silver four-by-four?'

"Of course." Dewi smacked himself on the head. "This could be Kenny's car. It still hasn't been found."

Dewi phoned for a vehicle check. His eyes shone as he turned to the DI. "It's Kenny's car. It's definitely his vehicle."

"And it's also a suspect vehicle in the hit and run. Call it in, Dewi. Get SOCO and uniform up here as soon as practicable. This place needs to be cordoned off." She turned towards Clive Jones. "We must ask you to return to your farm and wait to be questioned. This vehicle is potential evidence in two deaths. We must ask you not to enter this area again, until given the all clear by us."

"I've got work to do-"

"So have we, Mr Jones. So have we."

"Before I go, I don't know if it's connected, but someone scraped the gate up there with their car. At least, that's what it looks like to me. They left red paint on it."

"Really? Did it happen that night?"

"Can't say for sure, but it wasn't there before. It may have happened since."

Yvonne ran up to take a look. It definitely looked like a vehicle had been backing up towards the gate, possibly to turn their car around, or park up.

"Thank you," she said to the farmer. "I'll be down to speak to you, shortly."

After he had disappeared, Yvonne and Dewi took a few pictures, whilst waiting for further police and forensics to get there. The ground beneath the car was scorched, and the inside had been reduced to ash and melted frames.

"There's a large metal gateway over there." Dewi pointed to a farm gate. Designed to allow animals to move into the road, on their way to other fields.

"What's the road up there, Dewi? Is that the Dolfor road?"

Dewi nodded. "Near enough. It's actually part of the link road which runs between Dolfor and LLanbadarn Fynydd."

"The road leading to the moors? Where we thought Kenny may have met his abductor?"

"Right. Killer could have driven the vehicle down here, torched it, then gone back up to his own vehicle and driven away. And, Clive Jones is right. It wouldn't be the first vehicle to have been vandalised and left in this way. So, he wouldn't necessarily have felt it was urgent to tell us about it."

"Dewi, he may have been the man who torched it." The DI pursed her lips. It was then, she saw it. Chalked onto one of the wooden posts holding the gate. The Roman numeral for five. She ran over to it, quickly followed by Dewi.

"Ma'am?"

"Look, number five. Kenny was number five."

"Number five?"

"The fifth victim of our water-fetish killer. I'm now more convinced than ever that that is what we are looking at. I don't know if this vehicle is linked to the hit-and-run, but I strongly believe this is linked to the drowning of Kenny Walters. Safeguard this scene, Dewi, until the others get here. I'm off to interview Clive Jones."

"Alone?" Dewi raised an eyebrow.

"I've got mace and cuffs if I need them." She winked.

"I'll ask for someone to join you." Dewi nodded, reaching for his mobile phone.

"Clive Jones, you have the right to remain silent..." Yvonne recited the mantra to the farmer, who sighed and shook his head.

"Am I under arrest for telling you about a burned-out car?" He threw his cap down onto the large and battered oak kitchen table.

"Where were you, four nights ago?" Yvonne cast her eyes around the old farm kitchen. It had a certain charm, despite needing a good clean and a thorough update.

"Last Saturday?" Clive Jones kicked off his boots. His

thick socks had a ripe smell, and his big toes poked through holes. His toenails needing cutting.

Yvonne's eyes travelled back to his face. "Yes, Saturday night."

"Well, that's easy. I was out in town." He rubbed his back and reached for an old whistle kettle.

"Can anyone vouch for that?"

"Half the night-life in Newtown, I should think. Do I need an alibi? Do you think I torched that car myself?"

"We think that vehicle may have belonged to a drowning victim," she said, her voice deceptively soft.

"Wait a minute," Clive growled. "I didn't drown anyone. If you're trying to accuse me-"

"We'll be asking several people of their whereabouts."

"I'm not worried. Like I said, there are a lot of people who will tell you where I was." He reeled off a few names of friends and bar staff at the various places he'd been served drinks.

Yvonne noted them down. "Did you see anything suspicious around then? The day before? Saturday day time?"

He rubbed his chin, his eyes glazed. "Not that I recall."

"What about sound? You hear anything? Any noises in the night?"

"Nope. Nothing. Well, dogs were barking in the early hours, but that's nothing unusual. We get a lot of foxes roaming around up here. Tends to set the dogs off."

Yvonne made several notes. "There may be follow-up interviews with officers in uniform, and there will be a lot of police activity in your fields over the coming days."

He eyed her, as though looking for the words he wanted to say.

She waited, but there was nothing forthcoming.

37

COMNNECTIONS

Yvonne rapped the Chris LLewellyn's door. Instead of calling her in, as he would usually have done, he appeared at the door, causing her to step back in surprise.

"Is this a good time?" she asked, as he stepped back to allow her in. She wasn't sure why, but she had the feeling he had been pacing the room. He appeared pale, the lines deeper on his forehead.

"As good a time as any." He sighed. "I wanted to apologise to you." He leaned on his desk, part-seated. Legs triangulated with the floor.

"Oh?" She hadn't been expecting that.

"Yes. I think I was a little harsh, the last time you came to speak to me. Perhaps, a little too dismissive." He shook his head. "It's not easy making budget and manpower decisions, but that's not an excuse to stifle your ideas."

Yvonne's eyes searched his face. "About that, sir." She placed both her hands in the small of her back. "We have some developments."

He placed both his hands in his pockets, his eyes fixed on her face.

"We found Kenny Walter's vehicle burned-out, in some fields up above Dolfor. Not far from the Dolfor Moors. We haven't had full forensic analysis as yet, but we think it likely the car was torched the night Kenny died."

"And you don't think Kenny was responsible?"

"Well, we can't rule that out, but he would have had to walk back into town, before taking his own life...if that is what transpired."

"And, you don't think that is what happened, do you? I can see it in your eyes."

"No, I don't. I think his killer met him up there in order to buy drugs from him. Specifically, GHB. After the deal, I think he incapacitated Kenny, possibly by stabbing him with a syringe full of GHB, and then put him in his own vehicle, whilst disposing of Kenny's vehicle in a farm field. He doused it in petrol and set fire to it."

"Wow." LLewellyn thought for a moment. "Got anything to back that up?"

"Not forensically, yet. However, chalked on the field gatepost was a large Roman numeral for five."

The DCI frowned. "Five?"

"Fifth victim. If my concerns are correct, Kenny would have been the fifth drowning victim of a serial murderer."

"The Pusher..."

"Well, whatever you want to call him. It's not that simple, however. I don't believe he just pushes them in the river. I believe he drugs and abducts them first. I believe we have him on CCTV footage. We just don't have his face, and we don't have footage of him in the act."

"Do you think your killer is leaving a calling card? Chalking numerals for each victim?"

"I do."

"You need more than that, Yvonne. How do you know the markings you've seen are not just pointers for cross-country running or cyclists? Even treasure hunting?"

"I don't, for sure. And, I haven't found all of the numerals. But, I think they exist and we *will* find them."

The DCI grimaced, still having doubts.

"There's something else you ought to know." Yvonne sighed. "Kenny's vehicle is one of the suspect vehicles in the hit and run death of Callum Jenkins. I've asked forensics to examine for traces of blood and fibres. There was also some red paint, from another vehicle, left on the gatepost. Possibly unconnected, but we're looking into it."

Llewellyn's eyes narrowed. "Wait a minute, doesn't involvement in Callum's death give us more reason for why Kenny might have killed himself? Mightn't he have simply torched his vehicle and then walked into town to end it all? Perhaps he was wrestling with guilt all the way back into town."

"Can I at least look into this fully, sir? Give me the resources and I will find this killer and stop more young men from dying."

Llewellyn pursed his lips, his eyes searching those of the DI. "Alright," he said, puffing out a large volume of air. "Okay. I trust your instincts and I'm going to say go for it. But get me something, quickly. At least, give me some firm suspects. Someone we can interview. You can give this case equal priority to the hit-and-run. As soon as you have anything on that burned out vehicle, I want it, okay? We'll give a press conference. The community needs it and so do Callum's parents."

Yvonne nodded. "Will do, sir."

38

CAPTIVE

Yvonne found Callum and Dai having a quick coffee break. "Sorry to do this to you, guys, but could you check if either Rob Davies or Geoff Griffiths have a red vehicle? Oh, and could you let me know, ASAP?"

"But-" Callum looked down at his coffee and back.

"Yes, we can. No problem." Dai gave Callum a warning look. "What's the occasion, ma'am?"

She pulled a face, by way of apology. "It may be nothing, but it's possible that someone murdered Kenny Walters, and that someone deposited paint from their vehicle onto the gate, near where Kenny's car was found. It's a total long-shot, but it's all we've got at the moment."

"Sure, no problem." Dai led Callum out of the coffee area. They took their drinks with them.

Yvonne folded her arms, staring out the window, trying to make sense of everything in her head. Her mobile phone going off in her jacket pocket snapped her out of it.

"DI Giles?"

"Call for you, ma'am."

"Hello?"

"Hello? Is that Detective Inspector Yvonne Giles?" The voice was of a young female, and sounded hesitant.

"Yes. I'm Yvonne Giles. How can I help?"

"I was wondering if I could speak to Chris. Chris Halliwell. Is he with you?"

"PC Halliwell? I'm afraid he's not with me, no. He had to leave for a family emergency. He won't be back for a few days, at least. Can *I* help?"

"Um...Well, no. Not really. It's his daughter's birthday and she's been desperately waiting for his call. He usually calls her without fail, when he cannot be with her, on her birthday. We haven't heard from him."

"Wait." Yvonne frowned. "Who are you? Isn't his daughter in the hospital?"

"I'm Vicky, Chris's ex-partner and the mother of his daughter. His daughter's fine. She's not in hospital. She hasn't been to hospital in months. I don't understand."

"Vicky, when was the last time you heard from Chris?" The DI had become breathless, the words tumbling out.

"About four days ago. That is very unusual. He phones his daughter every evening. Without fail. I've tried contacting him but his phone is off."

"Oh." Yvonne's heart sank.

"What is it? Did he tell you he was going to the hospital?"

"There appears to be some sort of mix up. Don't worry, Vicky. I will get to the bottom of this and get back to you. Is it alright to call you back on this number, later?"

"Yes. Yes, of course. Is Chris alright?"

Yvonne bit her lip. "I'll find him and I'll get back to you.

Please don't worry, he may just have needed some time to himself. Please call us if you hear from him, okay?"

"Yes. I will." Vicky hung up.

Yvonne thought for a moment, tumbling through scenarios in her head. She ran to find Dewi and caught up with him on the stairs. "Dewi, find Jenny Hadley. Chris's family are looking for him. He hasn't been in touch. His daughter is not in the hospital." The DI fought to get her breath. "He may have told Jenny what he was really going to do. Maybe he's in his room in the hotel or..."

"Or?" Dewi looked at her, wide-eyed.

"Someone phoned him and told him his daughter was in the hospital. If so, then why? If he is not in his room, then he's missing and we need to find him."

Just then, Callum and Dai appeared. "Geoff Griffiths has a red car, ma'am. Rob Davies doesn't own a vehicle." Dai flicked his notepad shut.

"Right." Yvonne ran her hands through her hair. "Dai, Callum...PC Halliwell is missing. Speak to Jenny Hadley, find out if she knows where he is. If she doesn't, check his room at the hotel and inform the DCI that he is AWOL. Tell LLewellyn that Chris told me he'd had a phone call telling him that his daughter was in the hospital. He asked permission to go to her bedside and said he'd be a few days. Tell the DCI I'm very concerned." She turned to Dewi. "We're going to pay Geoff Griffiths a visit."

CHRIS HALLIWELL SPLUTTERED, *gasping for breath. He wasn't sure how much more he could take. Water had gone up his nostrils, in his mouth. His torturer had stepped back, as though*

having realised that Chris had taken as much as he could. The hood was pulled off his head, and Chris blinked, focussing on the ceiling and on his captor's face.

"Why?" he asked, still spitting water. "Why are you doing this to me? What have I done?"

"You keep asking that. The answer's not going to change. Some people like cycling or painting or playing chess. I like watching people drown."

"You..." The realisation dawned. "You're the person who's been killing young men. You're responsible for the bodies we've been fishing out of the river."

His gaoler clapped, slowly and deliberately, several times. "Clever boy. You might even make a detective, one day."

"Why?" Chris shook his head. "What do you get out of this?"

"Pleasure." His mouth curled into an evil smile.

"Are you going to kill me? Is my body going to be found in the river?" Since he'd seen his captor's face, Chris already knew the answer to his question but he asked it anyway.

"What do you think?" Again the evil, curling smile.

Chris fought against his restraints. There was no movement in them.

"Want some of this?" He held up a needle and syringe.

Chris eyed it, his breath catching. "No. No, I want to feel everything." He knew that if that syringe went in his arm, it would be the end. Whilst he was still conscious, there was still hope of an opening. "Don't kill me here. Kill me at the river. If I'm to drown, I'd like it to be in a natural environment."

His would-be killer laughed, putting down the syringe and placing both hands on his hips. "Nice try, PC Halliwell. Nice try."

The sound of a vehicle pulling into the yard startled the man. He stood stock-still and listened, cocking his head in concentration. The sound of doors shutting on the vehicle.

PC Halliwell opened his mouth to shout, but was punched full force to the side of his head. He was gagged, before the bag was placed on top of his head. He heard his captor retreat down the steps, closing the ceiling hatch. Hot tears covered his cheeks. He prayed it was the police and that they knew he was here. He prayed to see his little girl again. He prayed for a miracle.

SO CLOSE, BUT YET

Yvonne and Dewi were quickly out of the car, heading towards the open lock-up. A red Romero was inside and they gave it the once-over. There was no sign of the owner.

"Any sign of damage your side?" Yvonne's heart sank. There was nothing that she could see.

"No. Not a single blemish.'

"Damn." The DI took a quick look around the rest of the lock-up. Small tins of nuts and bolts, all labelled, boxes holding various tools, drill, hammer. Basic stuff. Nothing that could obviously be used to repair a vehicle.

A few old sacks, empty and folded, lay in a pile, and a stack of old paint tins and some paint brushes - none of them metallic paint and none in red.

"Maybe it's not him." Yvonne shook her head.

"Doesn't look like it." Dewi put his baton away. "Shall we talk to him anyway?"

"Yes. He's high on my list."

THEY HEARD footsteps running into the yard, crossing over to the lock up in just a few strides.

"You again?" He called to the officers inside.

Yvonne came out first. "We're checking local cars in the area. This yours?" She nodded behind her to the Romero.

"Yes, it is."

"A young boy was mown down two months ago-"

"I know...terrible. You haven't found the person who did it, then?"

"Not yet. You told me you use Maldwyn Sports Centre, right?"

"That's right. Why?" His eyes narrowed, he knew full well what she was suggesting.

"We think the person who killed him was a local, either resident or a user of the school or sports centre."

"Well, you've looked at my car, so you know it's not me, right? My car's red and he was killed with a silver car."

"Yeah." Yvonne tried to sound off-hand. She sensed something, she couldn't quite put a finger on. "Can we go inside for a chat?"

"Why?"

"Well, you use the sports centre, maybe you know someone who goes there, or you've seen something-"

"I haven't."

"All the same, a little chat wouldn't hurt. Anyway, I could murder a cup of tea."

There was sweat on his brow. He licked his lips, flicking a look up at a window at the top of the house. "Look, I do know something."

"Oh?" Dewi was at Yvonne's side, pocketbook open.

"I popped into Dingle Hall garage, around the time that boy was killed. I wanted to schedule a service for my vehicle."

"Go on."

"Well, there was someone else there...Kenny."

"Kenny who?"

"Walters...I think that's his name."

"Kenny Walters, the drug dealer who was found in the river?"

"Kenny had taken his car there to be fixed. A four-by-four. An old Suzuki, I think it was." He swallowed hard.

"Go on."

"I spotted some blood on the window. A smear. I pointed it out to Kenny and he looked panicked. Told me he'd hit a small deer. He washed it off, before the garage hand took the vehicle in."

"If you knew a young boy had been killed, why didn't you report this to the police?" Yvonne took a step towards him.

He scowled, as though he wanted to hurt her. "I guess I just didn't make the association, back then."

"So, when did you make the association?"

"Just now." The words were delivered slow and cold. "If you don't believe me, go down to the Dingle garage and ask them. Ask them if they carried out repairs on Kenny's vehicle. They'll tell you."

"We will." Yvonne was still staring at him, studying his face. He looked uncomfortable.

Her mobile interjected.

"DI Giles?"

"Ma'am." It was DC Callum Jones. "Chris's car has been located. It's at a garage at Halfway House, near Shrewsbury."

"Is Chris at the garage?"

"He's nowhere to be seen, ma'am. The garage owners called it in. They phoned West Mercia police to tell them that the car had been abandoned there. No-one has been in touch about it. They reported it as an abandoned vehicle."

"I see."

"There's something else."

"Go on."

"There was a rag stuffed in the exhaust."

"Sabotage…"

"Looks like it, ma'am."

Yvonne shot a look at Dewi. "We've got somewhere to be." She looked at Geoff Griffiths. "Are you working later?"

"Yes, I am."

"Then, we'll speak to you tomorrow." She wanted to stay. Stay and squeeze this witness like a sponge. But finding Chris Haliwell had to take priority. She narrowed her eyes at Griffiths before turning for the exit.

40

THE RAG IN THE PIPE

Yvonne, Dewi and Jenny Hadley piled into an unmarked vehicle and Dewi put his foot down, as much as he was able. The roads between Newtown and Shrewsbury were good but always busy. Still, they were at Halfway House in around forty minutes. The car had been dumped on the garage forecourt. Someone came out to greet them, cleaning his hands on piece of cloth.

"Is this it?" Yvonne walked around the back to examine the rag in the exhaust. She didn't touch it. She'd leave that to forensics. She crouched to get a better look.

"Obviously planned." Dewi crouched beside her.

"Looks like it, doesn't it? Well thought out, too. They didn't completely block the exhaust. Just hampered it enough to cause engine problems." She pointed to the some of the rag which protruded out from the exhaust. "This was done in the dark. The saboteur didn't have to worry too much about Chris, or anyone else, seeing this. If it had been done in daylight, the rag would have had to have been completely concealed."

"Whoever did this, likely followed him down here. Chris had engine problems and probably pulled over to take a look."

Yvonne nodded. "His abductor came up and asked if he needed help. Chris would have told him about his sick daughter."

"The sick daughter the abductor already knew about, as he'd made the call."

"Right. And he offered him a lift. Chris probably thought he could pick the car up from here another time."

"Walking straight into the trap."

"But who?" Yvonne turned to Jenny, whose eyes glistened, as she stood listening. "Jenny..."

"Yes?" She sounded choked.

"You've spent more time with Chris than anyone."

She nodded.

"Besides us, who knew that Chris has a daughter who occasionally gets sick and spends time in hospital?"

"Well I...I don't know...er."

"Did you see him tell anyone? Talk to anyone about it? Did he tell you that he'd talked to anyone? Did you talk to anyone?"

"Me? No. I wouldn't have talked to anyone about Chris's personal life. I don't think he...no, wait. He *did* tell someone about it. It was a casual conversation. We'd gone for a drink in the bar of the hotel we're staying in."

"The Elephant and Castle?" Dewi asked.

"Yes. The Elephant. Some guy was sat in there on his own. He came over to chat to us. We're talking a few weeks back, now." She looked from Yvonne to Dewi and back. "I can't remember everything that was said. I remember feeling uncomfortable about the way he had intruded on our conversation." She shook her head. " But, Chris seemed pretty relaxed about it. Like he felt sorry for the man."

"What did Chris tell him?" Yvonne's eyes were soft and encouraging.

"That he had a daughter that he didn't see as often as he'd like. I don't think he went into that much detail but he did tell him she had been hospitalised a number of times."

"Jenny, what was the man's name?" Yvonne's eyes were earnest but, she remained patient, keeping her voice steady and even.

"I don't recall him giving it."

"What did he look like?"

"He was dressed in dark clothing. Er, black trousers, White shirt and dark jumper. He was quite tall with dark hair, beginning to grey. A long nose. I remember a long nose. Dark brown eyes."

"Did he say he worked in a bar?" Yvonne's eyes had shrunk to pinpricks.

"Yes. Yes, I think he did."

"The Sportsman?" Dewi straightened up.

"It rings a bell."

"Geoff Griffiths." Yvonne ran back to the car. "Let's go, I'll drive. Dewi, get a call out to all officers in the Newtown area to be on the lookout. Get a duty assigned to the river and ask the DCI to get an ARV unit to Geoff Griffith's house as soon as practicable. We'll meet them there." She fired up the engine as the others clambered in. "Dammit!" She sighed, as the wheels span into motion. "Why the hell didn't we go into his house when we were there earlier?"

No-one answered. Dewi was busy making calls. Jenny sat in the back, in silent shock.

Yvonne whacked on the siren and blue lights.

41

RACE AGAINST TIME

Chris Halliwell had listened intently but had not heard anything of what transpired outside. When his captor returned to the house alone, all hope left him. It was some time, however, before the man came back to the attic. Sunken eyes followed him, as he heaved two watering cans over to the bed. Water sloshed everywhere.

The PC was sore from lying in his own filth. He could feel his bed sores oozing. He was nauseated and knew this man was going to kill him. He should probably just get it over with.

His captor dumped the two cans and grabbed the hood.

"You can't dump me in the river. You know that." Chris summoned up one last little bit of fight. "There isn't a scenario that would fit with this. I'm not a drinker. I don't take drugs. My car is in some garage somewhere and I have sores all over my body. No-one is going to buy accidental drowning."

"No one needs to. You'll be buried. Lots of wild places

around here. I doubt you'd be found for decades." With that, the hood was placed over his head.

Chris readied himself for the onslaught. He had thought that he might just breathe in the water. Get it over with. In the end, his body's reflexes kicked in. He spluttered, gurgled and fought against it, just as he had done previously.

IN THE GARDEN, a team of heavily armed and armoured men poured like ninjas from a police van, just prior to Yvonne's car arriving on scene. The DCI had also confirmed he was on his way.

The DI skidded to a stop behind a tall hedge and waited. She had a tight knot in her stomach, wanting to be in that house, now. She strongly believed that Chris was in there and she desperately hoped he was still alive. At least now, they had a chance of rescuing him. If he wasn't here? She didn't want to think about that.

She looked across at Jenny Hadley. Tears were streaming down her face. Yvonne realised, for the first time, that she must have feelings for him. She put an arm around her shoulders. "It's going to be alright", she whispered.

"Yvonne." The DCI was on her left shoulder.

She jumped and put a hand to her chest, her breathing fast. "Chris. I hope I've got this right. I'm sure he's in there. I'm sure he's been taken by a killer."

"I should have listened to you." The DCI placed a hand on her back. "Let's let those guys do their job."

Yvonne's eyes searched around. Dewi had gone back to the car, and was on another call. They moved to where they could see through the vegetation. "I don't see a negotiator."

The DCI shook his head. "They're going to storm the place. He doesn't have a gun licence and we've no reason to think he owns one. Once they're in position, it'll be all systems go. They know what they're doing."

Her gaze was back on the house. She marvelled at how silent and focussed, those heavily armed men could be. Well-trained and dedicated, they surrounded the house before forcing the door. She held her breath.

IN THE ATTIC, Chris had endured one of the watering cans. He was still spluttering, when he was ordered to shut up. He'd wet himself again. He felt wretched, but did as he was told and quietened down. He couldn't hear anything. The hood amplified his breathing.

Chris knew he was going to die. His torturer had not yet returned to his bedside. Was there someone down there? Were armed police looking for him? He called out, as loudly as he could. Muffled as the sounds were, they still carried a little until his captor hit him hard across the head with a blunt object, rendering him unconscious.

HE DIDN'T SEE the hatch smash up, as a heavily armed officer burst up the steps, followed by several more.

Geoff Griffiths put his hands up. There was no point in trying to run.

One of the heavily armed officers ran to the window and opened the curtains to signal to those in the garden. Another officer pulled the hood off Chris Halliwell and began reviving him. Ambulance staff ran across the garden with a stretcher.

Yvonne paced, biting on her fist. She couldn't settle until she knew the young PC was okay. Dewi was back with her, looking up at the house.

As the stretcher came out, she saw Chris trying to look around him, grimacing in pain. One of the ambulance staff carried a drip, attached the PC's arm.

"Thank God." Yvonne hugged Dewi, the DCI and Jenny Hadley. There were tears. They had come so close to losing one of their own.

"Well done." Dewi put a hand on Yvonne's shoulder. "You were right. You've saved more than his life." He nodded in the direction of the disappearing ambulance.

Geoff Griffiths was brought out in cuffs. His head hung down, he appeared a far cry from the vicious killer they knew him to be.

"I don't know if this is the right time." DCI Llewellyn addressed Yvonne, running a hand through his hair. "They found traces of DNA and fibres from Callum Jenkins in the grill on Kenny Walters burned-out car."

Yvonne turned to him, eyes glistening. "Kenny killed Callum."

"Looks like it. The garage confirmed that Kenny had taken his car to be fixed. They hadn't seen blood. Kenny must have wiped off anything obvious."

"I should talk to his parents." She nodded.

"Yes, but not yet. There'll be time tomorrow. You need rest. Hell, we all need rest." The DCI motioned to them all. "Come on, we're finished here. Let's let SOCO through to gather the evidence. I want Geoff Griffiths put away for a very long time."

The End

AFTERWORD

If you enjoyed this book, I'd be very grateful if you'd post a short review on Amazon. Your support really does make a difference and I read all the reviews personally.

Mailing list: You can join my emailing list here : AnnamarieMorgan.com

Facebook page: AnnamarieMorganAuthor

You might also like to read the other books in the series:

Book 1: Death Master:
After months of mental and physical therapy, Yvonne Giles, an Oxford DI, is back at work and that's just how she likes it. So when she's asked to hunt the serial killer responsible for taking apart young women, the DI jumps at the chance but hides the fact she is suffering debilitating flashbacks. She is told to work with Tasha Phillips, an in-her-

face, criminal psychologist. The DI is not enamoured with the idea. Tasha has a lot to prove. Yvonne has a lot to get over. A tentative link with a 20 year-old cold case brings them closer to the truth but events then take a horrifyingly personal turn.

Book 2: You Will Die

After apprehending an Oxford Serial Killer, and almost losing her life in the process, DI Yvonne Giles has left England for a quieter life in rural Wales.Her peace is shattered when she is asked to hunt a priest-killing psychopath, who taunts the police with messages inscribed on the corpses.Yvonne requests the help of Dr. Tasha Phillips, a psychologist and friend, to aid in the hunt. But the killer is one step ahead and the ultimatum, he sets them, could leave everyone devastated.

Book 3: Total Wipeout

A whole family is wiped out with a shotgun. At first glance, it's an open-and-shut case. The dad did it, then killed himself. The deaths follow at least two similar family wipeouts – attributed to the financial crash.

So why doesn't that sit right with Detective Inspector Yvonne Giles? And why has a rape occurred in the area, in the weeks preceding each family's demise? Her seniors do not believe there are questions to answer. DI Giles must therefore risk everything, in a high-stakes investigation ofa mysterious masonic ring and players in high finance.

Can she find the answers, before the next innocent family is wiped out?

Book 4: Deep Cut

In a tiny hamlet in North Wales, a female recruit is murdered whilst on Christmas home leave. Detective Inspector Yvonne Giles is asked to cut short her own leave, to investigate. Why was the young soldier killed? And is her death related to several alleged suicides at her army base? DI Giles this it is, and that someone powerful has a dark secret they will do anything to hide.

Watch out for Book 6 coming in the spring : Vanished Children

Printed in Poland
by Amazon Fulfillment
Poland Sp. z o.o., Wrocław